CATHY LEON...

At first Cathy's new job seems ~~Withdrawn~~ ~~come true.~~
She loves picking up the phon~~e~~ ~~is.~~ "This is
Cathy Leonard calling." For most people Cathy no
longer has to add that she is collecting society news for
her town newspaper, *The County Crier.* They expect
her call now. And when in the line of duty, Cathy even
manages to rescue a neighbor, her fame grows even
more.

Sometimes, however, Cathy must force herself to climb
the stairs and shut herself in with the telephone. Not
only is it hard to miss out on all the fun she could be
having with her friend Naomi, but she knows that she
is not spending as much time as she would like with
her little brother and sister, and that her grades are beginning to slip. Yet in spite of this, Cathy is still not
sure if she is ready to give up the job that means so
much to her.

"Miss Woolley's characters are so very real they climb
right off the page."

—*Chicago Tribune*

Cathy Leonard Calling

BY CATHERINE WOOLLEY

Puffin Books

PUFFIN BOOKS
Published by the Penguin Group
Viking Penguin Inc., 40 West 23rd Street, New York, New York 10010, U.S.A.
Penguin Books Ltd, 27 Wrights Lane, London W8 5TZ England
Penguin Books Australia Ltd, Ringwood, Victoria, Australia
Penguin Books Canada Ltd, 2801 John Street, Markham, Ontario, Canada L3R 1B4
Penguin Books (N.Z.) Ltd, 182–190 Wairau Road, Auckland 10, New Zealand

Penguin Books Ltd, Registered Offices: Harmondsworth, Middlesex, England

First published in the United States of America by William Morrow & Company, Inc., 1961
Published in Puffin Books, 1988 by arrangement with William Morrow & Company, Inc.
Copyright © Catherine Woolley, 1960, 1961
All rights reserved
Printed in the United States of America by R. R. Donnelley & Sons Company,
Harrisonburg, Virginia
Set in Garamond #3

Library of Congress Cataloging in Publication Data
Thayer, Jane 1904–   Cathy Leonard calling.
Summary: Ten-year-old Cathy enjoys being society
reporter for the local paper but soon finds out that
her position leaves little time for homework or family activities.
[1. Journalism—Fiction] 2. Schools—Fiction.
3. Family life—Fiction] I. Title.
PZ7.T3297Cat 1988   [Fic]   87-36135   ISBN 0-14-032551-4

CONTENTS

Cathy Leonard Calling

Cathy Meets the Editor

Cathy Leonard was the first one out of the fifth-grade door when the River View Consolidated School bell rang at three-fifteen.

"See you later!" she called over her shoulder to her friend Naomi. Cathy hurried down the corridor and ran out the open door, ignoring the school buses lined up to receive the approaching throng. Coat flying open, books and lunch box tightly clutched, she headed for the parking lot where she had seen her mother drive in.

Cathy climbed breathlessly into the seat. "Hi!"

"Hello." Mother smiled at her. "Shouldn't

you comb your hair and wash your hands before you call on Miss Hobway?"

"I washed them," Cathy protested.

"Give me your comb a minute."

Cathy produced it and submitted while Mother tidied her swinging, light brown hair, that curled a little at the ends. "There." Mother straightened the collar of her daughter's blouse. "Pull your jacket up. Now you look better."

"Oh!" Cathy breathed. "I'm so excited! I can't believe I'm going to be a newspaper reporter!"

Mother backed the car, and they drove out of the parking lot and headed toward Northvale, where Miss Hobway lived. Miss Hobway was the society reporter who sent news from the towns of Northvale and Middle Bridge to the *Ferris County Crier*.

"I'm so glad she's going to Florida!" Cathy went on. "Wasn't she simply adorable to ask me to send in the news while she's away?"

When they were on the road, Mother said, in answer, "It's going to be a lot of work for you."

"Oh, I don't think so." Cathy was too blissful about this wonderful job to have any worries. "I know millions of people, and I'll just ask them to tell me when they're going to have company, and stuff like that."

"We can't have it interfering with your school work."

"It won't. I got a hundred in arithmetic and spelling today, by the way."

"As usual." Mother smiled down at her.

Cathy nodded absent-mindedly. "Mother, you'll help me with the writing, won't you? Just at first, I mean."

"Yes. And Miss Hobway will tell you what you're supposed to do."

It was a drowsy October afternoon. A faint aura of burning leaves tangled in the mild, misty air. The oaks and maples in the yards of the white houses along the country road stood proudly arrayed in their scarlet and gold, and the yellow leaves covering the yards dazzled the eyes like sunshine. Why do people rake up autumn leaves, Cathy wondered briefly, looking out. They're so pretty.

Miss Hobway, gray-haired and comfortably plump, welcomed them out of the autumn brilliance into the dim coziness of her

5

little old house. "We're going to have a cup of cocoa," she said. "I know little girls are hungry when they get home from school. It's all ready."

"I'll help." Cathy followed her into the kitchen. She did want to help, but she had never been here before and she was curious to see the rest of the house. Cathy liked houses, just as she liked people.

"You take these cookies to the table." Miss Hobway poured steaming cocoa into a china pot and followed her to the dining room. "We'll just sit around the table. I can think better around a table, can't you?"

Mother and Miss Hobway chatted, and Cathy sipped the cocoa, feeling its warmth glow within her. She did not hear what the grownups were saying. She was dreaming again about being a reporter.

"More cocoa, dear?"

"No, thank you," Cathy said. "It was very good."

Miss Hobway removed the cups and came back with a pad of paper. "Now we'll get down to business. I've made a list of the things you'll have to do, and I thought we'd go right down the list." She looked at Cathy across the table. "Oh dear, you *are* very young!"

"But I'm very good in language arts," Cathy said quickly. "And I just love to write!"

Miss Hobway looked reassured. "You seem to have a nose for news. That's why I thought of you when we simply couldn't find anyone else." She adjusted her glasses and glanced at the paper before her.

"Well, anyway," she began, "the job is to send in a column of society news every week from Middle Bridge and Northvale. Now here's a list of names and telephone numbers. These are people who often have news. They have lots of company, and they go away, and so on. I call them fairly regularly. Of course"— Miss Hobway looked up at Cathy—"most of these people live in Northvale. I know Northvale better, because I live here. You live in Middle Bridge, so you'll know lots of people there to call."

"Oh, yes," Cathy said. "It's such a tiny place. And there are kids from Northvale in school. They'll tell me when they—when their parents, I mean—have company and everything."

Miss Hobway looked doubtful. "You'll have to be sure the names are spelled right, and get all your facts straight. It might be better to call their mothers."

"Oh, I will." Nothing could daunt Cathy today.

"The paper comes out on Thursday," Miss Hobway went on. "Your news must be in the office—that's in Springdale—by Tuesday at six P.M."

Cathy glanced at Mother. Here was one place where she would need help, for Springdale was six miles from Middle Bridge.

"We'll get it in," Mother said.

"I cut out some sample news items and pasted them on this sheet." Miss Hobway pushed a paper toward Cathy. "If you follow this general wording you'll be all right. Here are some envelopes. And here's how you address the envelope." An envelope came across the table. "Mr. Stark is the editor. Incidentally, he wants to see you. I told him you were young, but smart."

Cathy felt the color surge into her face.

"And I said that, with your mother's help, I thought you could handle the job. We had to have somebody to cover these two towns, and there wasn't another soul who would do it. Now, every month you send in your string. . . ."

Cathy's head was beginning to whirl. Miss Hobway explained what a "string" was. "You cut all your items out of the paper and paste them together in a string. You're paid by the inch."

It seemed unbelievable that she would be paid for something she wanted to do so much!

"Don't send anything except society news," Miss Hobway cautioned. "And do it all by telephone. Don't go running around, Cathy. You might get hurt or something."

"But if I happened to hear about some news—like a fire—couldn't I send it in?" Cathy asked.

"Indeed you may not!" Miss Hobway told her.

"O.K." Cathy was sorry she could not go rushing to fires, when the siren blew, and write stories about them.

They rose to go. "I hope it will work out," Miss Hobway repeated. "Mr. Stark has had so many problems since he took over that paper, poor man. I know you're terribly young. But go down and see Mr. Stark. This week's news is in, by the way, but you can start right in on next week if you want to, and if you have any trouble I can help you before I go."

Back in the car, Cathy clutched her papers. Her head was spinning and her cheeks felt on fire. "Whew!" she breathed. "I'm mixed up!"

"It will straighten out," Mother said comfortingly.

"Oh, I can hardly wait to tell Naomi." Cathy was silent for a few moments. Then she said, "Do you know why I really want to do this, Mother?"

"Why?"

"Because I want to be a foreign correspondent some day. And this will be good practice. Won't it?"

"I should think so." Mother glanced down at her wrist watch. "Chris and Jeff are probably wondering what's happened to us."

"Oh, they knew we were going to Miss Hobway's." Cathy dismissed her younger sister and brother. "They're probably in with Naomi."

The Leonards' old-fashioned home was so big that it housed two families these days. Naomi Hughes and her mother, who wrote books for girls, were the tenants in a three-room apartment on one side of the first floor. Naomi was Cathy's best friend.

"I want to pick up some vegetables," Mother said. She turned the car in front of a big roadside stand. At one side the ground was golden with a great spill of pumpkins.

"Oh, Mother!" Cathy cried. "Let's get a great big pumpkin, so we can make a jack-o'-lantern for Halloween."

When they reached home Mother drove around to the kitchen door. Cathy climbed out, bending to lift the heavy pumpkin from the floor of the car. She dumped it on the kitchen table, tossed her coat and books on a chair, and headed for the front hall and Naomi's door. She could hear Chris and Jeff coming downstairs, but it was Naomi she wanted to tell about her interview.

"Oh, Naomi!" She stooped to pick up Naomi's kitten and cuddle him against her cheek. "I'm actually, really and truly a reporter!"

Naomi and her mother were interested and

impressed. Later, when she went into the kitchen to ask Mother if she could go and see Mr. Stark tomorrow, Cathy heard six-year-old Jeff and Chris, eight, behind her. Jeff was lugging his kitten, Simon, and Chris had hers, named Wiggly.

"What's a reporter?" Jeff inquired.

"It's what Cathy's going to be," Chris explained. "They write things in the paper."

"Why?"

"I don't know. She just wants to."

Cathy set the table for dinner dreamily. Her feet were so light she felt lifted off the ground; her head seemed far up in the clouds.

At dinner she told Daddy all about the interview. Daddy did not show great enthusiasm. "Sounds like a big job at your age."

"Oh no. It's going to be easy!"

"Well, we'll see. If it's too much you can drop it."

"I can't drop it! I promised Miss Hobway. . . ." Cathy's eyes flew to her mother.

"Don't worry about it now," Mother said.

Cathy breathed freely again. "Anyway, it's not going to be hard. You'll see, Daddy." She pushed back her chair and went around to drop a fairy kiss on his forehead.

Next morning she told her friends, Martha McArdle, who lived next door, and Gretchen Lacy, as they all waited for the school bus. The girls were thrilled with Cathy's new role of reporter.

In school Cathy told Miss Riker. But her teacher's reaction was like Daddy's. "You're too young, Cathy! And you're my best student. I don't want this job to interfere."

"Oh, it won't." The doubts of grownups could not touch her.

She told Mr. Moore, the principal, and Mrs. Breck, his secretary, when she went to the office on an errand. She told Mr. Lippo, the janitor, when she met him in the hall. The janitor's response, at least, was heart-warming. "So? You're smart girl!" He beamed at her.

The next afternoon Mother picked her up at school again, and they went to Springdale. "I'll do a couple of errands while you call on your editor," Mother said.

The newspaper office was small and stuffy. The strong carbolic-acid smell of fresh ink greeted Cathy when she opened the door.

She sniffed it and liked it. From a larger room in the rear came the roar and pounding of presses. A man, whom she assumed to be Editor Stark, sat at a desk talking on the phone. He was in his shirt sleeves, and he held the telephone on his shoulder with one cheek, while he scribbled notes on a piece of paper.

"Right," he said into the phone. He hung up, pushing his pencil behind one ear. Then he glanced up at Cathy. Editor Stark was as lean as Miss Hobway was plump, and his dark hawklike eyes looked out of a sallow face. Cathy's heart stirred uncomfortably at the sight of him.

Cathy's pulse beat faster. "I'm Cathy Leonard."

The name appeared to mean nothing. His eyes strayed back to the sheet in his typewriter as if he was impatient at the interruption.

"Well, I'm going to be the new reporter while Miss Hobway's away."

Only his eyes, rolling up at her suddenly, revealed that he was startled. "*You* are?"

There was an unpleasant emphasis on *you*. Cathy felt her courage ebbing. "Yes." She tried to make it definite, but the sound came out of her small and faint.

He stared at her. "How old are you?"

"I'm ten and a half, almost eleven."

"Ye gods!" said Mr. Stark.

Cathy sought words to fill the uncomfortable silence. "My mother is going to help me."

"Oh no!" said the editor weakly. "Now I've heard everything. A ten-year-old reporter!"

"Ten and a *half*," Cathy said.

He shut his eyes and shook his head. He looked as if he were trying to make her disappear, Cathy thought, but she was still standing there when he looked again.

Suddenly he barked, "Well, do you know what you're supposed to do?"

She jumped. "Oh yes! Miss Hobway told me."

"Go and do it." He swung around toward his typewriter, then looked up briefly. "Nothing but the little social news you can get on the phone. Understand?"

"Oh, I know. No fires or. . . ."

"No fires." He repeated the words sarcastically.

She turned toward the door, only too glad to go. But suddenly, in spite of herself, curiosity possessed Cathy. Ready to run if he yelled at her again, she said, "Mr. Stark, would it be all right if I went in there"—she nodded toward the sound of the presses—"for just a minute? I'd love to see how they print the newspaper and everything."

The phone rang and the editor reached for it. "Go ahead," he said, as if resigned now to her being around. "But don't bother them in there."

Cathy tiptoed into the press room and stood silent, fascinated as the presses rose, pounced on the blank paper, and let the printed sheets slide into a pile. An old man nodded at her and came over to hand her a paper, fresh from the press.

"Thank you." She took it gratefully. "It's noisy here!" she shouted. She wanted to tell him that she was the new reporter, but she didn't quite dare to, with Mr. Stark in the next room.

When she came out, the editor did not even glance in her direction. Cathy went out on the street. Mr. Stark was so grouchy! She didn't like him at all, she thought. There were very few people she didn't like, but very few people had ever been as unpleasant to her as he had.

"How was it?" Mother asked as she climbed into the car.

"Fine," Cathy said.

"Did you like the editor?"

"He's—very nice." She could confide practically anything in Mother, but for some reason she wanted to keep to herself the sudden doubtful feeling about the job that crept like a chill along her blood.

It was not until they were out of town, riding along through the rich farmlands with the sun setting back of the hazy blue hills, that the comfort of this familiar scene began to reach her. Her low spirits stirred and began to climb toward their normal level.

Cathy sighed deeply and relaxed, and suddenly the old confidence flowed strongly back. It was going to be all right. I'm not afraid of that old Mr. Stark, she thought. I can do it! I know I can!

Society Reporter

When Cathy and Mother reached home, Cathy wasted no time in starting her new job. This was Wednesday, which meant that she had six days to prepare her first news. It might take a little longer the first time than it would when she got used to doing it, she thought.

"May I be excused from setting the table?" she asked Mother. "I'd like to make some phone calls and start getting news."

Mother was tying a fresh blue apron about her waist. "Chris may set the table tonight."

Chris came wandering into the kitchen, Wiggly in her arms. "You're going to set the table tonight, Chrissy," Cathy told her, departing.

"Why can't you help?" Chris cried.

Going through the dining room toward the hall, Cathy heard Mother explain. "Because Cathy has a job to do now, you know, and she's anxious to get started."

"Isn't she ever going to set the table again?"

"Oh yes, of course. She just needs a little extra time when she's getting started."

"Then Jeff can help," Chris announced.

Jeff was playing with his trucks on the dining-room floor. "I can not!" he shouted. "It's not my turn!"

Cathy went quietly upstairs to the telephone in Mother's room with her list of names, paper and pencil, leaving the argument behind. Mother had excused her, so her conscience was clear. She sat down on the bed. Now! With a comfortable feeling of getting to work at last, she consulted the list of names Miss Hobway had given her.

Here was one name in Northvale that she knew—Mrs. Richards. That was Diane Richards' mother. Cathy had gone to a party at her house. She picked up the receiver and dialed.

"Hello," Cathy said. "Hi, Diane. This is Cathy Leonard calling."

Diane was surprised to hear from her. "Oh," Cathy said with a chuckle, "didn't I tell you I was a newspaper reporter? A *newspaper* reporter!"

This called for a lengthy explanation. Finally she got Diane to call her mother and explained all over again to her. But after all that, Mrs. Richards had no news to offer.

Diane came back on the line and talked about school. At last Cathy said, "Well, I'd better stop talking. I forgot to ask your mother if she'll please call me when she has company or anything like that. Would you please take down my phone number, Diane?" After Diane had found a pencil and paper, Cathy finally hung up.

Well, she would try another name. She was astonished when Chris called up the stairs to say dinner was ready. She had made only two calls. They had taken a long time, and she had nothing whatever to show for it. Well, she told herself again, it would take time to get started, of course.

After dinner she picked up the dessert plates and followed Mother to the kitchen. "May I be excused from wiping dishes?"

Chris came in with glasses from the table and stood still in the middle of the floor. "What! Is she going to get out of wiping dishes *too?*"

Mother looked from one of her daughters to the other and shook her head, smiling a little. "You'll have to work out a schedule, Cathy. Of course you can't be excused all the time. But go ahead now. It's all right, Chris. Don't be so indignant."

This time Cathy felt like staying downstairs where the rest of the family was, so she settled herself at the phone in the hall. She made three calls, and on the third try she learned that Mr. and Mrs. Robert Garside were going away for the weekend. She wrote it down carefully and then, jubilant, hung up the phone with a clatter and went bouncing into the living room, where Daddy was reading the paper.

"I've got my first society news!" she cried, waving the paper. She read it to him, wording it according to the sample Miss Hobway had given her. "Isn't that *beautiful?*" She covered her face with the paper and spun around.

"Very fine," Daddy said. "Are you going to be on that phone all evening?"

But Cathy was on her way to read Naomi her news.

"That's good, Cathy," Naomi said. "Come on in and do homework."

"Oh, I can't! I have to make more phone calls."

On the next call she got another of her classmates, and a long conversation followed—but no news. She had just hung up when Jeff came into the living room and turned on the television.

"Jeff!" Cathy shouted. "Please turn that down. I can't hear!"

"I want to watch cowboys!"

Mother came in. "Go up and use my phone, Cathy."

As Cathy gathered up her papers, she heard Daddy say, "Is she going to be on the phone all night every night? I'm not sure this job is a good idea."

Cathy softly closed the bedroom door. She

made two calls, and they were lucky ones, each producing a suitable item of news. But suddenly her eyes fell on the clock. It was nine o'clock and she had done no homework. I'll get up early and do it, she thought. Anyhow, I've got three news items!

Mrs. Wolf in Northvale was going to visit her mother. What a sweet voice that Mrs. Wolf had, she thought. And Mr. and Mrs. Smith were having friends in to play bridge. She had something for future use, too. Mr. and Mrs. Fox were going to have their tenth wedding anniversary on November twenty-fifth and were planning to celebrate by giving a dinner party. That would make lovely news when the time came. How funny, she thought. I've got Mrs. Wolf and Mrs. Fox!

She jotted a note on a scrap of paper, *Don't forget! Tenth Anniversary Party Nov. 25.* She could remember the rest. Cathy lay back on Mother's bed, gazing blissfully at the ceiling, her society news clutched in her hand.

She slept restlessly that night. It was hard to open her eyes in the morning, but she had set the clock for six. She sat up and turned off the alarm blindly, groping her way into her bathrobe. She did her arithmetic half asleep.

She and Naomi almost missed the school bus, but Cathy was awake by now. She felt happy and gay and was laughing when they climbed aboard. At the back of the bus Gretchen was saving seats for them with a group of their classmates.

"I have an announcement to make!" Cathy stood in the rear of the aisle dramatically. "I am now a society reporter for the *Ferris County Crier*! And *you* are all going to help me!"

Martha and Gretchen and Naomi promised co-operation. But Gloria Graham said curiously, "Why are you a reporter?"

"Because—well, somebody asked me to be one. And I want to. Will you all please let me know whenever your mothers have company or anything, so I can put it in the paper?"

Bernice Judd spoke up. "Do you get paid?"

Cathy nodded happily.

"So," Bernice said, "we're supposed to give you the news. Who's going to pay us?"

Cathy was taken aback. To her the money

part of the job was unimportant. The knowledge that she would be paid something for her work was there, pleasantly, in the background. But the big, wonderful thing was that she was writing for a newspaper. Ever since she had known Naomi she had wanted to be a writer, especially a foreign correspondent. Mrs. Hughes wrote books, and Naomi's father, no longer living, had been a foreign correspondent at one time. Naomi had lived in Paris.

Writing was a thrilling, wonderful thing to do, Cathy thought, and it opened the doors of the whole world to you. She could not get over the miracle of having this opportunity to write fall into her lap.

"Well," she said, her gaiety subdued a little, "you'll get your name—or your parents' names—in the paper. It won't cost you anything."

This seemed to give Bernice food for thought, but she was not accepting Cathy's new honor with grace. "So?" Bernice said rudely.

"We'll help anyway, Cathy," Gretchen said. "Won't we, Marcia?"

Several voices chorused, "We will too," and Cathy felt better. Her spirits bubbled again, and she laughed and chattered the rest of the way to school.

She told Miss Riker that she had several society items already. "That's good," the teacher said. "But remember—you're not going to let it interfere with school!"

"Oh no!" Cathy promised.

Suddenly she thought of how sleepy she had been this morning when she had dragged herself out of bed to do homework. But she drew a shutter across that picture. The job was bound to take a little time at the start, she assured herself again.

At recess Gretchen said, "Cathy, I just happened to remember that my mother is going to have a meeting of the church circle at our house. Do you want to put that in the paper?"

"Yes! Oh dear, I haven't got any paper or pencil. But I can remember. When is she having it?"

"Monday."

"O.K. Oh, what's your mother's name?"

Gretchen gazed at her in astonishment. "Mrs. Lacy!"

"I mean, what's your father's name?"

"He's not going to the circle!"

Cathy giggled. "I know, but I have to write, 'Mrs. John Lacy,' or something."

"Oh. My father's name is George."

"Then I'll say, 'Mrs. George Lacy was hostess to the Circle. . . .'"

"She *wasn't*. She's *going* to be, I told you."

"But the paper comes out Thursday, and by that time the meeting will be over."

"I couldn't ever keep it straight!" Gretchen said, marveling.

Naomi and Marcia had come up to hear the end of the conversation, and Naomi said, "Well, Cathy, you'll know if we have any company, anyway."

"My mother is going to the garden club this afternoon, I think," Marcia said.

"Where?"

"I forget."

Cathy gave a small sigh. Getting news from her school friends was not going to be quite as simple as she had thought. "Kids," she said, "when you give me news will you please find out everything about it? If you don't, I'll have to call up, and it takes so much time."

Marcia said she would ask her mother about the garden club. As the bell rang and they all headed into the building, Bernice caught up with Cathy. "You said you wanted news," she said. "Well, my father is going to a farm managers' convention, if you want that."

Cathy hesitated, uncertain. "I don't *think*," she said after a moment, sorry she had to say this to Bernice, "that what men do is society news—unless ladies go along."

"Oh." Bernice sounded miffed. "O.K., you don't have to use it."

"I can send it in, though," Cathy said hastily. "They might print it."

When Cathy and Naomi got home from school that afternoon they were greeted at the door by Chris and Jeff. "Mother said we could make fudge for Halloween!" Chris cried. "We're going to put it in the bags. Will you help us, Cathy?"

Tomorrow was Halloween. Cathy loved Halloween, and she was very fond of fudge, and it was not easy to say no to the eager children. "I ought to do some telephoning," she began.

They wailed, and Chris complained to the world, "Cathy can't set the table or wash dishes or make fudge or *anything* any more!"

"She can't do anything but telephone dopey people!" Jeff shouted.

"I'll help you, Jeffy," Naomi said. "I'll just change my dress first."

"And I'll hurry," Cathy promised.

She ran upstairs. I won't waste a bit of time, she thought. I'll make a lot of calls quickly and then go down.

By four-thirty she had obtained two more news items. I'd better call Martha about the garden club, she thought. But Martha's mother was not yet home from the meeting, and in spite of herself Cathy got into a long conversation with Martha, who had things to say about what a mean girl Bernice was. That reminded Cathy to call Bernice and find out more about the farm convention, even though she was not sure that anything a man did was society news.

As she hung up after making that call Cathy paused to sniff. The rich, dark aroma of chocolate fudge was in the air now. Mm! There was another smell too—popcorn! They were popping corn down there.

It was getting dark, and she did not feel like making any more calls now. Cathy thought of homework, but brushed it aside. She was starving, and she couldn't do homework on an empty stomach. She went flying downstairs, her muscles rejoicing in action.

Naomi, Chris, and Jeff were sitting on the floor in front of the fire in Naomi's living room, a plate of fudge on the hearth. Chris's small face looked fire-flushed, and chocolate ringed Jeff's mouth. Naomi was shaking a popper full of softly exploding kernels over the glowing coals.

They were delighted to see her. "I'm going to be a cowboy for Halloween!" Jeff shouted.

"I'm going to be a gypsy. Naomi's going to help me," Chris added. "What're you going to be, Cathy?"

Cathy threw herself on the floor and helped herself to fudge. "I don't know." She gazed dreamily into the fire. "I may not have time to dress up. News takes quite a long time to get." She was scarcely aware of the small sigh that escaped her.

Naomi said wistfully, "Will you have to work on your job every single day and night?"

"Not when I get used to it," Cathy assured Naomi and herself at the same time, taking another piece of the warm, delicious fudge.

"I hate to do homework alone!" Naomi said fiercely.

"Oh, we can still do it together. I'll have loads of time after I get started." But somehow homework did not seem important to Cathy right now, not compared with the job of getting news for the *Ferris County Crier*. She supposed she would have to do some homework before tomorrow. Some time. . . .

Cathy stretched flat and put her head on her arms. What luxury! She would like to stay here forever, looking into the fire.

And then the little flame of eagerness, mirroring the flame on the hearth, sprang to life within her once more. She was a reporter. She wanted a good column of news to send in. After dinner she would go upstairs very quietly, so Daddy wouldn't hear her and think

31

about her using the telephone. Or even before dinner, if Chris would set the table. If she could get two or three more little news items tonight. . . .

Jeff said, "Daddy's going to make a jack-o'-lantern tonight."

Good, Cathy thought. Then Daddy wouldn't notice that she was telephoning again. "That's nice, Jeffy," she said. "He'll make a real good one for you, and we'll put it in the window."

Trick or Treat

As Cathy and Naomi came out of school Halloween afternoon, crowds of sprites in costume and mask were swarming into the waiting buses. The younger children had been having parties.

Cathy chuckled, waiting for the little children to climb into the bus. "Don't they look cute," Naomi said.

Cathy nodded. "Chris and Jeff were going to wear their costumes to school this afternoon." The younger Leonards did not attend River View School, which needed to be enlarged to accommodate all the children in the district. Their classes were held in the smaller, older school in Middle Bridge.

Cathy had just settled into a seat when Gloria got on, looked over the bus until she spotted Cathy, and paused by her seat. "If you want some news," she said, not too graciously, "we're going to have company Sunday."

"Oh!" Cathy searched in her bag for pencil and paper. "What are their names?"

Gloria was prepared with all the information. "Thank you very much," Cathy said.

When Gloria had gone on to the back of the bus Gretchen leaned across the aisle. "She just wants to get her name in the paper!" she whispered.

"Sh!" Cathy shook her head warningly. Whatever the motive for offering the news, she was glad to have it, and she was grateful for a sign that she might expect help from this quarter after all.

Chris and Jeff were busy at the dining-room table when the girls got home, filling bags with popcorn and chocolate fudge to hand out to trick-or-treat guests. Jeff was wearing his cowboy suit. Chris had not been able to get her gypsy outfit ready to wear to school. "But you're going to help me to-night," she reminded Naomi.

"Oh dear." Cathy sighed, laying her books on a chair. "I suppose I've got to start tele-phoning." She almost added, "I wish I didn't have to," but caught herself in time. She did not want anyone to think she regretted taking on the job of reporter, because she didn't for one moment. It was just because of Hallow-een, she told herself. It was hard to remove herself from the fun.

But she was still far from having enough news to send in, so, resolutely, she forced herself to climb the stairs and shut herself in with the telephone.

It was a bad time for news-getting. Every-one seemed to be out on this beautiful Friday afternoon, and after half an hour Cathy gave up, glad of an excuse. I'll phone some people around dinnertime, she thought, and ran downstairs.

"Look, Cathy!" Chris came into the hall to meet her, pointing to a table by the front door. "See all the bags we've got ready!"

Jeff suddenly rushed to the door. "I see

some kids coming up the road!" he shouted. He pulled open the door and rushed onto the front porch.

"Can-dy!" he yelled at the top of his lungs. A cluster of ghosts, tramps, and pirates accepted the invitation and turned up the driveway. Chris and Jeff bestowed bags of treats.

The jack-o'-lantern was ready in the kitchen. As dusk came on, Cathy carried it to a front window, and Mother touched a match to the candle inside. The soft yellow glow blossomed, bringing the grinning features into bright relief. The smell of melting wax stole upward with the warmth of the flame, and all the children ran out on the porch to get the effect through the window.

More Halloween spirits arrived at the door, stowed their treats in bulging bags, and trotted off down the drive.

"Jeff," Chris said, "we ought to go out, or everybody's treats will be all given away."

"O.K.! Let's go!" Jeff cried.

Feet pounded on the steps, and another delegation rang the bell. Chris was terribly torn between being there to bestow bounty and going out herself to get some. Finally she decided to get into costume. She and Naomi and Cathy went into Naomi's living room to get her ready, while Jeff tended the door.

"Cathy," Chris said, submitting to having various colored sashes tied around her gypsy dress, "aren't you coming with us? You always come with us on Halloween!"

"I don't know," Cathy said.

"You've got to, Naomi, if Cathy won't," Chris insisted, "because you're bigger, and after it's dark Jeff and me can't go alone."

"Jeff and *I*, Chrissy," Cathy corrected. She sat back on the floor and admired her sister's costume. Naomi was covering Chris's soft, fair hair with a bright bandanna. Gold rings dangled from Chris's small pink ears. "Oh dear," said Cathy. "I don't know whether to go or not! I ought to telephone some more. I haven't got much news. I'll rush up and call some people now before it's time to go out."

She could not bear to miss the Halloween fun: the cool dark filled with the damp, earthy smells and windy rustlings of fall; the mysterious figures looming up in the night; the welcome at lighted doors; and the treasure trove of waiting treats. Cathy's pulse quick-ened at a sudden memory of how a mask felt on her face—hot and a little scratchy and smelling of cloth and glue.

She had an idea! She gave a small gasp of delight, then clapped her hand over her mouth.

"What's the matter?" Naomi asked.

"I just thought of something. Let's go with the kids, Naomi! I'm going up and get ready, and you get ready too!" She scrambled to her feet and went flying up the stairs to her room.

Tucked into the back of Cathy's mind all along had been plans for what she would wear on Halloween, for really, it had been unthinkable that she would not take part. Now she took the old evening dress of Mother's, that she loved, from her closet and got a chair to stand on and find the silver slippers on a high shelf.

Arrayed in her finery, she tiptoed as softly as the high heels would permit into Mother's room and applied rouge and lipstick liberally.

Then Cathy went back to her own room and proceeded to carry out the details of a plan which had come to her earlier. Carefully she tore several sheets of paper into small pieces. On each slip she wrote her name and telephone number. She laid the pile of slips in readiness on her bed and added a pad of paper and a pencil.

The doorbell rang again as she went carefully down in her high heels, and a cold draft swept through the sheer dress when Jeff energetically flung open the door. There were very few bags left on the table.

Cathy went on into the kitchen. "How do I look, madam?" she said mincingly to Mother.

Mother looked her over and laughed. "You look simply charming—your highness!" she retorted. "Only, if you will kindly permit me, I shall rearrange the rouge."

Cathy found a tissue and lifted her face, and Mother removed and blended rouge and blotted up excess lipstick.

"Now you look as pretty as a picture," Mother announced. "Why don't you take the children out for half an hour before dinner— just next door and across the street?"

"O.K." Cathy was only too happy to do so.

"Aren't you wearing a mask?" Mother asked.

"Just a half mask. That goes best with my dress." She did not mention that the half mask fitted in with her plan as well as with her costume.

Naomi was dressed as a witch. "You look wonderful!" Cathy cried.

"You look beautiful!" Naomi replied admiringly.

"Oh, I know what, Naomi," Cathy exclaimed. "Why don't you take one of the kittens? Witches always have cats."

"Yes," Chris said. "Only take one of ours, Naomi. Maybe you could give her to somebody, because I want a parakeet, and Mother says I can't have one as long as we've got three kittens!"

"O.K., I'll take Independence."

Simon, Wiggly, and Independence were underfoot, as usual, and Naomi scooped up the latter and dumped him into her empty bag. They all laughed, until Mother said, "Is that sanitary?" Then they laughed some more, and Naomi decided to leave Independence behind.

As they were leaving, Cathy hesitated. But her plans could wait until they went out again after dinner, she decided.

The four trooped down the drive. It was

dark now. The strong tang of bonfire smoke stung Cathy's nostrils, and the wind whisked the leaves crisply across the lawn. There was a moon, but seas of clouds rolled heavily over it.

They went next door to Martha's and to two houses across the street and to Gretchen's, over near the post office. Then it was time for Daddy's bus, and they trailed home, bearing a worthwhile burden.

"There's Daddy going in. And there's a gang just going up our drive," Cathy said, standing still. "Chris and Jeff, you run ahead and go with them. See if Daddy recognizes you."

She and Naomi trailed behind as the crowd of children, Chris and Jeff in their midst, rang the bell. Mother, with Daddy behind her, opened the door upon the lighted hall, and the visitors poured in. Cathy waited a moment, then opened the door.

"Do you know these children?" Mother was saying, laughing, to Daddy.

He looked them over and shook his head. "Never saw one of them before."

Jeff and Chris jumped up and down, and

Jeff shouted, "It's me, Daddy! And that's Chrissy! We fooled you!"

Dinner was a hasty affair, with the children, in costume, too excited to eat. Daddy said, "I'll take you down the road in the car and wait while you make your calls."

Cathy was almost out the door again, as eager as the others, when she exclaimed, "Oh, I forgot something. Wait for me!"

She climbed the stairs as fast as her high heels permitted, seized the slips of paper she had worked on that afternoon, and was stuffing them into her bag as she descended again.

"What are those for?" Mother inquired.

"Just something." Breathless, she stood on tiptoe to kiss her mother, then hurried after the others.

Daddy let them out at the edge of the village. Mr. and Mrs. Stewart's house was first, and they trooped up the walk and rang the bell. Mrs. Stewart had a plate of cookies ready, and Jeff helped himself so liberally that Cathy whispered, "Don't be piggy, Jeffy!"

He looked guiltily at Mrs. Stewart. "You take all you want," she told him.

When the others turned away from the

door, Cathy lingered for a moment. She reached into her bag and said quickly in a low voice, "Mrs. Stewart, I just wanted to tell you—I'm Cathy Leonard." She raised her brief mask hastily to show her face. "And I'm a society reporter for the *Ferris County Crier* now. Here's my telephone number on this piece of paper. Would you please call me up if your daughter comes to visit you, or anything like that, so I can put it in the paper?"

She turned to hurry after the others. "Oh, by the way, can you think of any news right now?"

Mrs. Stewart couldn't. She was sorry.

"Oh, that's all right," Cathy assured her, and tripped off on her silver heels.

Across the street Mr. and Mrs. Robbins invited them in, to be admired and plied with bags of goodies. Again Cathy sought an excuse to linger. "I have to fix my shoe," she said to the others. "Go ahead."

She produced one of her calling cards and made her little speech. "I'm Cathy Leonard. I'm a society reporter for the *Crier* now. Here's my telephone number in case you have any news."

At the third house Chris discovered a parakeet and gave a little moan of longing. "Oh, you're beautiful!" She put her finger into the cage and talked to the bird tenderly.

Here, too, Cathy had a piece of luck. When she handed over her telephone number, Mrs. Lindstrom said, "We have a friend coming to spend Sunday."

"Oh good!" Cathy dived into her bag for pad and pencil. "I'll be right out, kids!" she shouted, and took down the name of Mrs. Lindstrom's friend. "That's wonderful. Thank you!"

Mrs. Mann lived next to the Lindstroms, alone except for her collie, Angus. She accepted Cathy's phone number. "I go to my daughter's quite often. That's about all, my dear."

"Are you going soon?"

Yes, Mrs. Mann was going to visit her daughter soon. Pad and pencil came out, and Cathy carefully spelled the name of Mrs. Mann's daughter.

"Oh, thank you!" she said. "Well, goodby. 'By, Angus. Does Angus go to your daughter's with you?"

"Oh yes. Wherever I go Angus goes."

Cathy paused before the next house. "Mrs. Denny lives here," she said doubtfully. "She's Gretchen's grandmother—or *great*-grandmother, I think. She's very old. Should we go there?"

"Her light is on," Jeff pointed out optimistically.

Not only was Mrs. Denny's porch light on, but she was ready for them with candy bars. The old lady was deaf, they knew, so they did not try to talk much. She patted Jeff's head, admired Cathy's and Chris's finery, and showed a proper terror of the old witch.

When the others had gone down the walk, however, Cathy decided to make an effort, at least. She raised her mask. "Mrs. Denny, I'm Cathy Leonard," she said loudly. "See, you know me."

"Why, you're Gretchen's little friend." The old lady beamed at her.

Cathy nodded. "I'm a reporter for the paper now."

"How's that?"

"Re-por-ter. I am going to put—things—in—the—paper."

"You want some paper?"

"No!" Cathy shook her head. "I'm going to write" . . . she made scribbling motions . . . "news!"

"You want a pencil? I've got one right. . . ."

"Oh no." Cathy gave up. "Never mind, Mrs. Denny. That's all right. Good-by! And thank you!" She ran after the others, giggling a little at her efforts to explain herself to Mrs. Denny. She's a nice old lady. I'm awful to laugh, she told herself.

When they got home they pulled off their masks, hot and sticky now. How good the air felt! They poured their loot on the dining-room table. Jeff counted four apples, two chocolate bars, eleven packets of assorted candy, gum, sourballs, lollipops, and cookies. Also seventeen cents.

"Good heavens!" Daddy said, as more and more "treats" appeared from the seemingly bottomless depths of their bags. "We can open a store!"

There was not room for everything on the table. Cathy turned her bag upside down on the floor and dumped the contents in a heap. Pencil and pad, with scribbled notes, fell out with the rest. She glanced up to see Mother's eyes on her again, and turned the pad face down.

"I'll explain later," she said softly.

She wanted to keep the little secret of doing business that evening. If she told Daddy, he might think that if she couldn't take one single evening off for fun the job really was more than she could handle. And she must never, never let him think that!

Because it wasn't. It was fun. She had gotten three social notes tonight just as easily as anything. Her column was coming along nicely, thanks to this evening's efforts. And now loads of people in Middle Bridge had her telephone number and had promised to call her. Practically all she had to do, she was sure, was wait for them to call and give her news.

Cathy hummed happily to herself as she lugged her loot upstairs and stowed it away on the shelf with the silver slippers, where Jeff could not possibly come upon it.

In the Paper

Cathy got her society news ready to send in on Tuesday afternoon. Mrs. Hughes lent her her typewriter. Cathy set it on the dining-room table, and surrounded by sheets and scraps of paper, she began to assemble her news column.

Jeff came in eating a banana and stood breathing down her neck. "What are you writing on the typewriter?"

"Get away." She waved him off as if he had been a mosquito.

Chris appeared. "Cathy, why do you have to write everything on the typewriter?"

"Because I do. Will you please go out! Climb a tree or something. And take Jeff."

"Come on, Jeff." Chris spoke in a low voice. Cathy could tell she was trying to co-operate. "Cathy's very busy."

Between typing with two fingers and stopping to consult her samples and see how the items should be worded, it was slow going. She had filled one sheet of paper when Mother came downstairs. "How are you doing, dear?" Mother asked.

"Oh, all right. Only it looks awful!" Cathy made a face at the sheet in the typewriter.

"Let me see." Mother held the sheet up. "Why, I think this is fine! It's very good for the first time, Cathy! Is this all?"

"No, there's some more."

"Would you like me to retype it when you finish, just so it will be extra neat the first time you send it in?"

"Well. . . ." Cathy would have preferred to do it all herself, but perhaps, she thought, it would be just as well to make a good first impression on Mr. Stark. "O.K.," she said. "When I get the rest typed."

There were almost two pages of society news from Middle Bridge and Northvale when she finished. Mother made a few penciled changes and typed the items over. Cathy enviously watched her fingers fly. Mother had taken typing in school, so she could type her papers in college. It looked so easy when she did it.

"There!" Mother pulled the second sheet from the machine.

"Oh, thank you." Cathy took the sheet and studied the two pages. She was very much pleased. "I really did all the work except the second typing," she said, reassuring herself.

"You certainly did. All those phone calls. And you actually wrote all the news yourself."

Cathy gathered her papers. "We'd better go now." Two scraps fluttered to the floor, and she stooped to pick them up, glancing at them. "This is just to remind me about Mrs. Wolf's anniversary." She tucked it under a paper clip. "Oh," she said, reading the other, "this is that one Gloria gave me. I forgot to put it in. Is there room on the paper?"

Mother typed Gloria's news at the bottom of the sheet. Cathy folded the two sheets of paper, typed the envelope as Miss Hobway had shown her, and followed Mother out to the car.

She had hoped the newspaper office would be closed, so she could push her copy through the mail slot. She was not eager to meet Mr. Stark again. But the place was lighted, and the editor was busy at his typewriter. She went in, her heart beating uncomfortably.

He glanced up, scowling.

"Hi," Cathy said nervously. She tiptoed to the desk, feeling she must not bother him, and held out the envelope. "I'll just leave this."

But he reached for it, slit the envelope with a paper knife, and glanced down the two sheets. He gave a grunt. "You type this?"

"Well, my mother really typed it over. But I did everything else." She hesitated, poised for flight but yearning for reassurance. "I hope it's all right," she said politely.

He tossed the sheets on the cluttered desk and swung back to his typing. "I'll tell you any time it isn't."

Was that all he had to say, after all her hard work? "Well, good-by," Cathy said bleakly.

She left without a further word from the editor.

What a mean man, she thought, walking back to the car, all her joy gone. If she didn't want to be a correspondent so much, she would tell him to find his own old society reporter!

But she did want to be a foreign correspondent some day.

Mother looked at her as she climbed into the car. "Was it all right?"

"Oh yes." She didn't want to talk or think about Mr. Stark.

In spite of the surly editor, Cathy's spirits rebounded and her expectations soared in the next two days as she looked forward to seeing the *Ferris County Crier* when it came out. She could not believe that the words she had written would appear in the paper. She wouldn't believe it until she saw it! In the background was a sickening feeling that, although she had heard no complaints from the editor, he might just leave out everything she had written.

The Leonards' paper always arrived in Friday's mail. "Let me get it, please, Mother!" Cathy begged. "I can't bear to have anyone look at it till I see if my news is there!"

She got off the school bus at the post office on Friday. "Don't come with me, Naomi," she said. "I just have to look at it alone!"

Mrs. Rouse, the postmistress, pushed the mail, including the paper, over the counter. "Oh," Cathy breathed. "I can't wait to see the news I wrote in the *Crier!*"

Mrs. Rouse nodded at her. "There's quite some pieces about folks in Middle Bridge."

"There are?" Cathy cried.

"You write those?"

"Yes! At least I think I did." She wouldn't believe it until she read it with her own eyes.

Standing at the counter, she ripped the wrapper from the paper. She turned the pages, glancing over each. It was not on page two . . . not on three . . . not on four . . .

Then she saw the Middle Bridge headline. Cathy's eyes raced down the column. There they were: Mrs. Garside, Mrs. Wolf, the Lindstroms, Mrs. Mann, the church circle. . . .

She gave a great sigh, folded the paper hastily, and headed for the door.

"Don't you want your other mail, Cathy?" Mrs. Rouse called.

Cathy turned, beaming, the paper hugged to her chest. "Oh, I can't believe it! That darling, wonderful, adorable Mr. Stark! He put my news in the paper!"

At home, she took the paper to her room, after showing it to Mother, and shut the door to enjoy it at leisure. Everything looked so important in the paper, she marveled.

At last she went downstairs. Chris and Jeff came in, rosy and panting, and helped themselves to Halloween candy from a dwindling supply on the sideboard.

"Jeffy," Cathy cried, "do you want to see what your darling sister wrote in the *County Crier?*"

Jeff made a face. "Crummy old paper!"

She looked at him in surprise. "Jeff!"

"That's not very nice, Jeff," Chris said reproachfully.

"Well, it is a crummy old paper. Cathy's always telephoning up people instead of playing with us."

Chris shook her head at him. "Jeff, you don't understand. When you have a job, you have to work. Daddy works hard in his job."

"He's a vice-president," Jeff said.

54

"Cathy might be a vice-president some day, too."

"No, she won't. She's a girl."

Cathy stood smoothing the folds of the paper. She had not realized that Jeff felt this way about her job. Then Chris said, "Cathy, come on out in the orchard. There's millions of apples, and they look rotten. But Martha said they taste good, and they do. They taste like baked apples."

"I can't . . ." Cathy began.

"But you never do play with us any more!" Chris cried.

How could Cathy explain the flame of eagerness burning inside her? Now that she had seen her own work in print she could not wait to put together another column of news even better than the first one. But she looked at Chris's little face, flushed and frowning with hurt, and suddenly Cathy relented. "All right, I'll come out."

Naomi appeared as they trooped out the front door. "Oh," she cried, "Wait for me!"

They went around to the old orchard behind the barn, Chris and Jeff running ahead, delighted to have Cathy with them. Chris stood on tiptoe and reached to pluck one of the brown, wrinkled apples, handing it to her sister. "Taste it! Martha says they taste like that because they've been frozen."

"Ugh!" Cathy said, making a face.

But Chris was eating one herself, and finally Cathy took a small bite. Sure enough, soft and sweet, it tasted just like a baked apple.

Jeff said, "Come on and rake leaves, Cathy. Daddy said if we raked them he'd make a big, big bonfire!"

The children were excited and happy. "This seems just like old times, doesn't it, Jeff?" Chris cried.

"Old times!" Cathy said in amazement.

"Yes. Like when you used to do everything with us."

"But. . . ." Cathy was about to remind them that she had been a society reporter for only a little over a week. She had had no idea her brother and sister felt this way. She had been so absorbed in getting news, she had assumed that her family and friends were as delighted about her new job as she was. Of course, she knew Daddy did not quite approve, but he had said nothing more. Anyhow, she would have to forget the paper this one afternoon.

They found rakes and heaped the rustly leaves into great mounds. Cathy liked the cold damp smell that rose so strongly when the matted leaves were turned up. Jeff and Chris jumped into the dry piles, and Cathy and Naomi covered them like the babes in the woods in the fairy tale.

When they went in, Mother said, "What pink cheeks you have, dear!"

"I'm starving," Cathy said. "Oh, that looks good!" Mother was drawing a delicious-smelling meat loaf from the oven, and Cathy stooped to peek in at a pan of scalloped potatoes.

She didn't feel like telephoning anyone now. She wandered into the living room and stretched out on the sofa, picking up a favorite book. How good it felt to be lazy after that exercise and fun. The paper was just out, so surely she was entitled to one free evening. This was Friday, too, so homework was no worry. Oh, but it feels good to do nothing, she thought again, wriggling into the pillows.

Chris came in. "I'll set the table tonight, Cathy." She was feeling kindly, because Cathy had spent the afternoon with them.

"O.K., I'll wipe the dishes." Cathy opened her book. She hadn't read anything for ages—not since she had started to work for the paper. What a lovely feeling. . . .

Cathy looked forward to school on Monday. All the girls would have read the paper, and they would be pleased at seeing their mothers' names. She climbed onto the bus with a copy of the paper in her bag to show Miss Riker what she had written. There was a happy smile on her face. Martha and Naomi and Gretchen had already rejoiced with her, and Cathy felt rather like a heroine.

Bernice and Gloria sat in their usual places in the back. They were gazing out the window and both their noses, it occurred to Cathy, pointed straight up at the sky. Cathy's smile froze slightly. "Hi," she said.

They glanced at her, then turned quickly back to the window. Cathy looked questioningly at Martha and Naomi as they all slid into the long seat beside the other two. Gloria and Bernice put their heads together in a whisper.

"What's eating them?" Martha asked in a low voice.

"I don't know," Cathy said. But even as she spoke, an uncomfortable suspicion leaped into her mind. Suddenly she was sure that the news Bernice had given her about the convention was not in the paper.

Then, for the first time, she realized something else. The item Gloria had given her—the one Mother had typed at the end—had not been printed either! She had not missed it until now.

Cathy sat silent with dismay. Oh, that *would* have to happen! She had been afraid that the one about Bernice's father was not right to send, because Miss Hobway had not mentioned news about men. As for the other, she didn't know why it had not been used. Maybe there hadn't been room. She was sorry, but she had sent them both in, so it wasn't her fault. They needn't be mad at her!

Some of the happiness drained out of Cathy. She sat quietly looking out of the window as the bus stopped and more chattering children streamed in to fill the seats. What should she do—say she was sorry? That it wasn't her fault?

As they got up to leave the bus she let Martha and Naomi go on. Gloria and Bernice stared straight ahead stonily. "I'm sorry the news you gave me wasn't in the paper," Cathy said. "I sent it in."

She could see they did not believe her. They exchanged looks. "Well, you can just get your own news," Bernice retorted.

"We won't give you any more," Gloria added.

Righteous indignation flowed through Cathy. "You don't have to," she replied with dignity, and left the bus, her head high.

She had hoped to gather a new batch of news from her schoolmates today, but now she was not in the mood. Of course, she thought, it *would* be the two touchy and unfriendly girls whose news got cut out! She didn't even feel like showing her column to Miss Riker.

The teacher spoke to her, however. "Cathy, I'm glad to see you had a hundred on your arithmetic paper today. Last week you had one wrong almost every day."

"I know." Cathy regretted those errors.

"Don't let that job of yours come first!"

"Oh, I won't!" Cathy promised.

She had done her homework more carefully over the weekend. But she must be more careful every day, she told herself, and not do it hastily in the morning.

The fine edge of her enthusiasm was still dulled when she went home. Naomi said wistfully, "I wish we could do homework together."

"I'll have to do some telephoning first," Cathy replied. She could feel Naomi's loneliness as her friend went into her apartment and closed the door. She was not feeling happy herself. Homework with Naomi would be fun, but her copy was due again tomorrow night. Goodness, but the week rolled around fast, she thought.

Mother was reading a letter when she went into the living room. "What do you think?" she said. "Grandma Godfrey is coming to visit us."

Grandma Godfrey was Mother's mother.

She lived in Chicago and had never visited them in Middle Bridge. "She is? When?" Cathy asked.

"For Thanksgiving. She's coming east to visit your great-aunt Jessie in White Plains, and she'll stop here on the way for a few days."

Jeff had come in from the kitchen, cookies in both hands and crumbs on his face. Chris followed. They both sat down, munching.

"Grandma Godfrey's coming to visit us," Cathy said.

"Do I know her?" asked Jeff.

"You haven't seen her since you were a baby," Mother told him.

"Why is she coming?"

"Why, she wants to see us."

"Is she coming alone?" Jeff persisted.

"Yes," Mother said.

"How can she?"

"Why can't she come alone, Jeff?" Chris inquired.

"She's old, isn't she?" Jeff said. "Mike's grandmother is a million years old." Mike was Gretchen's brother, so Jeff had Mrs. Denny in mind.

Mother and Cathy laughed, and Mother said, "Grandma isn't quite as old as that. . . . Is that my cake burning?" She sniffed and hurried into the kitchen, while Cathy, Chris, and Jeff discussed the coming event.

"She'll have to sleep in the guest room," Chris said. "Did we ever have a guest before—to sleep, I mean?"

"I don't think so," Cathy said. They had not lived in Middle Bridge long.

"Well," Chris went on with satisfaction, "we ought to make it extra nice, because she's our grandmother and everything. I'm going to put my rosebud quilt on her bed, because it's nice and warm and cozy."

Jeff tried to think of something warm that he could contribute. "Simon can sleep with her. He's as warm as toast."

"She can have Wiggly too," Chris said quickly. "Only I *wish* we could find homes for Simon and Wiggly and Independence, so I could have a parakeet!"

Cathy giggled. "Sillies! As if Grandma wanted two cats sleeping with her!"

But as the others were considering Grandma's comfort so seriously, she wanted to be in on it. She went out to the kitchen. "Mother, I've got that pretty blue wool scarf that I hardly ever wear. Do you think that would make a nice cozy little shawl for Grandma to wear if she feels chilly?"

Busy with her cake, Mother said, "Lovely." Cathy went back to the living room.

"If she needs a cane or anything," Chris was saying, "I know where one is. I saw it in the attic."

"But I'm going to help her go up and down stairs!" Jeff cried.

"Good." Chris nodded approval.

Cathy suddenly felt cheered up. What pleasant excitement to look forward to. Perhaps she could take Grandma her breakfast every morning on the pink-flowered tray. She would help Grandma prop herself up with pillows, and put the shawl over her shoulders.

"Oh!" she exclaimed suddenly. She had just thought what a lovely society item Grandma would make. "I can put it in the paper! What's Grandma's whole name? Anyway, I can say, 'Mrs. Grandma Godfrey is visiting her son-in-law and daughter, Mr. and Mrs. Philip Leonard. . . .' "

"What's a son-in-law?" Jeff asked.

"Daddy is," said Cathy.

"He is not!" Jeff shouted indignantly.

"Oh, Jeffy, he is too!" Cathy burst out laughing. She headed for the stairs. Suddenly she was in the mood again for being a society reporter.

Grandma Godfrey

The last golden leaf was gone from the trees now, for November was half over. Gazing out the window as she sat at the telephone in the afternoon, Cathy could see the misty blue hills beyond the orchard. She could hear Chris and Jeff playing outdoors, and she often saw Naomi run across the lawn to study with Martha next door.

Cathy experienced a queer combination of feelings. She missed being with Naomi. Naomi was her dearest friend, and up to now they had been inseparable. Homework had been a cozy time of giggling and gossip, along with the work. Now Cathy did her schoolwork alone before she went to bed.

Sometimes, seeing the girls outdoors together, it was all she could do not to run downstairs and out the door to join them. But the fascination of pursuing news—even these little bits of society news—kept her doggedly at the phone, adding one more item, and then one more, to her list.

At school Miss Riker spoke to her again. "You missed three problems this morning. What's happening to you, Cathy?"

Worry furrowed Cathy's brow. "Well . . . my newspaper job takes quite a bit of time. But I do my homework very carefully!"

"When do you do it?"

"At night. I have to do my telephoning in the afternoon. Daddy doesn't like me to telephone at night." She did not add that sometimes it was quite late when she got around to homework.

Cathy was upset. It was a matter of pride with her to be at the head of her class. That afternoon she said to Naomi as they walked home from the bus, "How about doing homework?"

Naomi was delighted. They spent the afternoon together, and it was just like old times. Before dinner, with schoolwork out of the way, Cathy asked Mother if she could be excused from setting the table, so she could do just a tiny bit of telephoning.

"Cathy, it isn't fair to make Chris do all the work," Mother told her.

She did not make an issue of it, because then Mother might say she would have to give up the newspaper work. No, Cathy thought, as she set the table, there was no other way than to make her calls in the afternoon. She would just have to stay wider awake and get those old arithmetic examples right at bedtime.

She sighed deeply, as she placed knives and forks. It took so much time to get just a little bit of news. She could not rely on her friends at school at all, she reflected. They forgot, or they didn't get all the information she had to have. Oh well, Cathy thought, her spirits rising from momentary depression, I'll manage.

Meanwhile there was Thanksgiving to think about, and Grandma's visit. The children were busy getting ready. The guest room was prepared.

"I'm going to yell very loud when Grandma comes," Cathy heard Jeff announce to Chris. "Mike has to yell at his grandmother, and sometimes she doesn't hear him even then."

"That's because grandmothers are old. I'll yell too," Chris agreed.

Frost sparkled on the roofs in the early mornings when they went down to the bus. The grass stood stiff and white in the cold. Cathy loved the fuzzy warmth of her winter coat under her chin these crisp mornings, and the good clean smell of the wool.

Grandma was due to arrive the Monday before Thanksgiving. "Are we going to the station to meet her?" Jeff inquired one night at dinner.

"Why, she's driving," Mother said.

"How can she drive?" Jeff was astonished.

"Why can't she?" Mother inquired.

"She's old!"

But Grandma was driving, in a Volkswagen. And when Cathy got off the bus the Monday before Thanksgiving, there was the little gray Volkswagen, with an Illinois license, parked in front of the house.

There were voices upstairs. Cathy ran up

to the guest room, where Grandma was unpacking, surrounded by an admiring audience.

Cathy remembered Grandma, but she had forgotten how pretty she was. Grandma was small and dainty, with hair so fair that if there was white in it, the white did not show. She wore a violet-colored tweed suit, and her eyes were deep blue. She welcomed Cathy with a warm hug.

Jeff sat on the bed with a large and shining red truck before him, and Chris was holding a doll. "She's Grandma, Cathy," Jeff announced, pointing. "She brought me a truck. And she's got a Volkswagen and she's going to take us for a ride in it."

"She likes parakeets," Chris continued. "She might get me one if we get rid of the kittens. And she's going to take us to some very nice restaurant for dinner while she's here!"

Grandma hugged everyone again and produced a lovely pleated wool skirt, her gift for Cathy.

"Now, children," Mother said at last, "come on out and let Grandma rest. She's had a long drive today and she's tired."

70

"Oh, but I'm not one bit tired," Grandma protested. "This bag is unpacked. I'll put it in the closet." She opened the closet door and, putting the suitcase away, eyed a pink bed jacket hanging there. Cathy glanced quickly at Mother. It was Mother's new one, that she had never worn.

"I thought Grandma might need it," Cathy explained hastily. "I just borrowed it from you, Mother, because it's nice and warm."

"That's quite all right," Mother assured her.

"I also put a pair of bedroom slippers in the top drawer, Grandma," Cathy went on. "They're yours too, Mother, that you haven't worn yet."

"I'm glad you're taking care of Grandma," Mother said.

"And look, Grandma," Jeff cried, scrambling off the bed. "Here's a heating pad in the drawer. And a cane's in the closet, in case you need it." He remembered something. "Grandma!" Jeff shouted. "Can you hear all right?"

"I certainly can!" said Grandma, putting her hands over her ears.

"Oh. Chris and I were going to yell if you

couldn't. But you're nicer than Mike's grand-mother," he added, brightening up. "Isn't she, Chris?"

Chris nodded. "Yes. Mrs. Denny is very nice too, Jeffy, don't forget. She gave us chocolate bars."

"Grandma gave me this truck." Jeff patted the shiny red vehicle lovingly.

Grandma laughed and hugged him. "Well, anyway, thank you for all these perfectly wonderful things you've provided for me! I'll need every one!"

"And I'll bring your breakfast up," Cathy said.

"I'd adore it, darling."

It was very pleasant to have a grandmother who arrived bearing wonderful gifts, and who showed such gratifying appreciation of all their plans. Very satisfactory. Cathy hummed happily as she went into Mother's room and settled herself at the telephone.

She had to take her news in tonight, because tomorrow Mother was giving a tea for Grandma and could not take her to Springdale. She prepared to get the job out of the way in a hurry.

For once, everyone she called was home. By five o'clock she had gone down the list and had a respectable column of news. She was gathering her papers to take downstairs when she picked up a note that fluttered to the floor. *Don't forget! Tenth Anniversary Party. Nov. 25,* she read.

Cathy consulted her calendar. Wednesday was the twenty-fifth. Good, she thought, I can finally send that in—the Wolfs' anniversary party. She put it with the other society notes and ran down to type them.

Cathy ran all the way from the bus next day to get her dress changed before the ladies arrived for the tea. Chris was changing too, and trying to prevail on Jeff to put on his Sunday shirt and suit.

"No, sir!" Jeff threw himself flat on his face on the floor.

"Well, Mother said you could stay upstairs if you didn't get dressed up, so there, Jeff!" Chris told him. Jeff kicked the floor.

Cathy's new skirt and her soft blue sweater looked very pretty, she thought. She ran downstairs. The dining table was laid with the lace cloth and a centerpiece of bronze chrysanthemums and yellow candles. The silver teapot stood at one end, the coffeepot at the other. There were white and yellow mints and salted nuts in silver dishes.

The rich fragrance of coffee hung in the air. In the kitchen Mother was uncovering plates of tiny sandwiches and little frosted nut cakes and chocolate brownies.

The bell rang and Cathy ran to open the door. Ladies came. Mrs. Hughes and Martha McArdle's mother sat opposite one another at the table and poured. Candlelight flickered, and the sun, dropping low, threw shafts of gold across the room.

Chris came down and after a while a very pink Jeff, in his Sunday best, followed her, unable to resist the party. The talk grew in volume. Chris and Jeff circled the table, inspecting sandwiches closely and helping themselves.

"I thought I made so many cucumber sandwiches!" Mother said in the kitchen, filling the plate again.

Cathy held her peace, but carrying in the replenished sandwich plate, she whispered to

Chris, "Stop eating all the cucumber sandwiches!" Chris looked at Jeff and they giggled. Cathy shook her head at them sternly, but she tried a cucumber sandwich herself before she passed the plate again, and it tasted delicious. She took another.

She kept thinking happily of the news item she had written about this party. *Mrs. Philip Leonard gave a tea for her mother, Mrs. Charles Godfrey of Chicago, who is a guest of Mr. and Mrs. Leonard until after Thanksgiving.* Cathy felt at peace with the world today. She had got a hundred in arithmetic. She was in a lovely glow from Mother's candle-lit tea. And there was more gaiety to come as long as Grandma stayed.

Besides, society items seemed fairly easy to get right now, especially when she could send in delightful news about Mrs. Charles Godfrey.

Wednesday night Grandma took them all to dinner at a restaurant called the *Country Kitchen.* They were being seated at their table when Cathy spied familiar faces across the room. Mr. and Mrs. Gray were on her telephone list. Mother noticed the Grays, too, and nodded a greeting.

"Those people with them are Mr. Gray's sister and her husband," Cathy murmured. "They live in Buffalo. They came to spend Thanksgiving. They've got a new grand-child—boy, I think. Only I couldn't put that in the paper—the baby—because he's in Buffalo."

Her eyes brightened as they wandered to another table. "Oh, there are Mr. and Mrs. Lindstrom and Mrs. Lindstrom's cousin. Her name is Mrs. Davis. They haven't seen her for two years."

"Come on, Miss Gossip Column," Daddy said with a chuckle. "What are you having for dinner?"

They had roast beef. When Chris consulted the menu for dessert she said, "It says here 'Children's Menu.' Why does it say that, Daddy?"

"That's a special menu just for children. It's what you and Jeff had."

Jeff scowled. "Why?"

"Because you can't eat as much as a grownup."

"I can too! I could've eaten seventeen times as much roast beef!"

"We'll order it right away," said Daddy. "I don't think you'll be able to eat any ice cream and cake, of course."

Jeff hesitated. Then the scowl vanished, and he and Daddy grinned at each other, man to man. "I'll have ice cream," Jeff decided.

Cathy said dreamily, "Can I say in the paper that Mrs. Charles Godfrey took us to dinner?"

"You've had the Leonards in the paper enough," Mother told her.

They had eaten early, and people were standing in line for tables when they left. As Cathy was passing a pleasant-looking couple, the woman said something to her husband, and Cathy thought, I've heard that lady's voice. She's somebody I've talked to on the phone.

"Your table is ready, Mr. Wolf," the hostess said.

That was Mrs. Wolf! Cathy was pleased that she had recognized the voice and also that she was eating at a restaurant frequented by all these people in her society column.

Then suddenly she stood stock still. But—the Wolfs were having a dinner party. Wasn't that tonight? For a moment she felt confused. Certainly it was tonight, the night before Thanksgiving. What were they doing eating at the *Country Kitchen* all by themselves?

Or—*was* it the Wolfs who had the anniversary? She had written it down quite a while ago. And then Cathy gave such a horrified gasp that a man turned to look at her.

"Come on, Cathy," Mother was saying at the door of the restaurant.

Slowly Cathy followed her family out to the parking lot. But after the others had gotten into the car she stood there, her hand clapped over her mouth.

"What's the matter?" Mother asked.

"I made a terrible, horrible, awful mistake!"

"What?" Daddy demanded.

"I sent in a society news item about the Wolves'—Wolf's—anniversary."

"Well? Get in, Cathy," Daddy said.

She climbed in. "It wasn't the Wolves—Wolfs. It was the Foxes!"

They were all dismayed and sympathetic,

although Cathy, happening to glance at Daddy, felt suddenly suspicious of that look on his face. It was the look he wore when he was trying hard not to laugh. Well, it isn't funny, she thought hotly, almost ready to cry!

They discussed what to do. "Maybe it's not too late," Daddy suggested. "Why don't we drive around to the newspaper office and see?"

Cathy moaned. How could she face Mr. Stark? She sat silent and miserable as Daddy turned the car toward Springdale.

The editor apparently worked late. He was at his desk as usual when she walked in, and the presses were pounding. He glanced up, a flicker of surprise in his eyes, as she entered. "Well! What brings you out on this holiday eve?"

She might as well get it over quickly. "I did something *awful!*" Cathy said fiercely.

"You did?" Mr Stark leaned forward, resting his arms on his desk, and regarded her with interest. "What did you do—murder your grandmother?"

"No. I got the—the Wolves—Wolfs—and Foxes mixed up, and it's in the paper. And the *Foxes* were the ones, only I said the

Wolves—Wolfs. And I could just *die,* unless there's time to. . . ."

"Just a minute." The editor stopped her. "These animals. I don't get it."

"Not animals. They're married people! Only it was the Foxes' anniversary and dinner party, and I said the Wolves—Wolfs. And then tonight I saw Mr. and Mrs. Wolf at the *Country Kitchen,* and suddenly I knew. . . ." Cathy was horrified to feel a large sob rise up and shake her chest . . . "knew I'd. . . ." She stopped, looking down at her hands.

It was a dreadful moment. Mr. Stark looked down too. He looked very serious and drew designs on a piece of paper while she collected herself. After a while Cathy gave a sniff.

"That's too bad." The editor still did not look at her. "Reporters are supposed to get their facts straight."

"Is there time to change it?"

He shook his head. He moved a paperweight on his desk. "What do you think we ought to do?"

Cathy sighed shakily. "I guess—I'd better call up and explain."

"You do that," said Mr. Stark.

He was still staring down at his desk and making marks on a paper when she left. He seemed to feel just terrible about it, Cathy thought, badly shaken herself. He hadn't yelled at her, as she had expected, but he had acted so queer, and there was the strangest expression on his face.

She decided to wait until morning before calling the Wolfs and the Foxes. Cathy went to bed as soon as she got home, not in a mood for sociability. Just before she fell asleep, Mr. Stark's face, with its puzzling expression, floated up into her consciousness. Suddenly she thought, he almost looked the way Daddy does when he's trying not to laugh! But of course nothing could have been further from Mr. Stark's mind than laughter at her dreadful mistake in the paper. Cathy pulled the covers over her head.

The Wolfs and the Foxes were nice about her error when she called them in the morning. No serious damage done, they both said. A great weight rolled off Cathy's breast.

"That was a lesson I'll never forget!" she said to Mother.

Mrs. Hughes and Naomi came to Thanks-giving dinner. After dinner Daddy and Cathy and Chris and Jeff went for a ride with Grandma in the Volkswagen to show her the countryside.

They went home in the wintry blue dusk to turkey sandwiches and cocoa in front of Naomi's fire. Jeff sat on the sofa with Grandma. He was Grandma's boy now. "I wish you'd stay here forever," he told her.

"I wish I could." Grandma drew him close. "But I have to go tomorrow. Aunt Jessie is expecting me."

"I want to go with you," Jeff annnounced.

"Why can't he?" Cathy asked. "There isn't any school tomorrow. He could spend the weekend."

Jeff sat up in sudden interest.

"That's a wonderful idea!" Grandma said. "He could skip school Monday, couldn't he? I could bring him down to New York on the train Monday afternoon and take him to your office, Phil."

"Oh boy!" Jeff's eyes were big with ex-citement. "On the train? May I?"

But Mother shook her head gently, smiling at him. "Not this weekend, honey."

"Why not?"

"Well, for one thing, you've outgrown all the shoes you own, and some of your clothes, and I'm planning to take you shopping Saturday."

"I don't want to go shopping!" Jeff shouted.

"Jeff," Daddy said.

"Well, I don't. I'm not going, either!" Jeff's voice was loud and indignant. His chin quivered.

Naomi reached over to pat his hand. "You can go to White Plains some other time, Jeffy."

"Could he go next weekend?" Chris put in anxiously.

"How would we get him up there, Chris?" Mother asked.

"No," Daddy added. "Jeff will just have to wait until we drive up some time."

"We'll plan it soon," Grandma said comfortingly, putting her arm around Jeff.

But he drew away, threw himself down on the sofa, and pulled a pillow over his head to indicate his bitter disappointment.

"Come on, son," Daddy said. "While I think of it, I'm going to go out and put a new washer on the kitchen faucet. You can hold the tools."

After a while Jeff got up, his face still red and cross, and followed Daddy into the kitchen.

They saw Grandma off in the morning. "Come up soon," she said. "Jessie only has one extra bedroom, so you can't all come at once. But do come!"

"We shall," Mother assured her. "And you'll be here for Christmas."

Grandma gave Jeff an extra hug and kiss. "Jeffy, darling, come and see Grandma."

"When?"

"Ask Mother and Daddy to bring you soon. Good-by, Chris darling . . . Cathy honey." She was in the car. She waved. "Good-by." The little car bounced down the drive, turned into the road, and disappeared from sight as the Leonards waved.

Jeff ran into the house. Cathy couldn't bear to have him feel bad. She followed, to find him lying on the floor in his favorite posture of protest or despair.

"Don't cry, honey." She knelt to pat her

small brother's back. "You can go visit Grandma some time."

"No, I can't!" The muffled wail sounded heartbroken. "I'll never go!"

"Yes, you will. Cathy will fix things so you can." How, she didn't know, but she wanted to console him.

She was rewarded after a moment by a small sniff. Jeff was comforted. He trusted her.

"There. Now you're all right, aren't you?" she said.

He nodded, his face still hidden, restored to hope once more. Then he raised himself. "Cathy, play with me."

She hesitated. She ought to do some telephoning, she thought. She was behind, on account of all the festivities during Grandma's visit. But right now Jeff needed her.

"All right, let's play croquet," she said, and they went outdoors hand in hand.

More Trouble

"Cathy," Naomi said that afternoon, "know what? I've got ten subscriptions in the magazine drive. Martha's got nine. Have you got any?"

"Not yet," Cathy said.

Every year the pupils of River View School conducted a drive for magazine subscriptions. The money they earned went toward paying the expenses of the eighth grade on its spring trip to Washington. The drive had been on since early November, but with her newspaper job and Grandma's visit and Thanksgiving, Cathy had had no time to solicit subscriptions.

"I'll get some," she added.

"You'd better hurry," Naomi warned. "The drive is only on until Christmas."

The fact that she had contributed nothing toward the success of the drive did bother Cathy's conscience. One of these days she would be in the eighth grade and go to Washington with her class, and right now she ought to be helping the present eighth graders pay for their trip.

"I think I'll go make some phone calls for news now," she told Naomi. "If I get that done real quick, I'll go out on my bike and try and get some subscriptions."

It still gave Cathy pleasure to call up and say, "This is Cathy Leonard." For most people she no longer had to add, "of the *Ferris County Crier*," although she liked the sound of that, too. People knew her. They expected her call now.

It still gave her a tingling little thrill to see her news in print. Mr. Stark had never complained, so aside from the unfortunate episode of the Wolfs and the Foxes, which she had now banished from her mind, she thought she must be doing acceptable work.

The job was beginning to be routine, however. She always knew what was coming. There was Garden Club twice a month and the Women's Circle on Fridays and Mrs. Owen's bridge club on Tuesday and Mrs. Mann's visits to her daughter.

Cathy wished someone would do something exciting for a change. Or I wish I could write real articles about things, not just little snips about people having company, she thought impatiently.

She sat down to work this afternoon, consulting her list rather indifferently. Well, Mrs. Johnson in Northvale usually had some news. She dialed the number. If she could get three or four items quickly, she would devote the rest of the afternoon to the magazine drive.

Then suddenly, as she held the telephone, an idea blossomed full-blown in Cathy's brain. Why not, she asked herself, kill two birds with one stone? Why not ask Mrs. Johnson right now if she would like to subscribe to some magazines?

Mrs. Johnson was home. She said pleasantly that she and her husband were having some friends in Saturday night.

"Oh, thank you," Cathy said and took down

the names. She wasted no time. "Mrs. Johnson, by the way, we're having a magazine drive
in school for the eighth-grade trip to Washington. Would you like to subscribe to some
magazines?"

Mrs. Johnson was a nice woman. She waited
while Cathy ran to get her magazine list. She
said that she subscribed to several of these
publications but had an idea the subscriptions
were running out. Cathy assured her that re-
newals counted too. Mrs. Johnson promised
to put a check in the mail and Cathy hung
up, triumphant.

This was a positively gorgeous idea! She
giggled to herself as she proceeded to dial
Mrs. Riggin. Won't Naomi be surprised when
I tell her I've got a lot of subscriptions, she
thought delightedly. What a *brilliant* idea!

Mrs. Riggin gave her a news item but
seemed rather cool to the magazine idea. "It's
to help the eighth grade," Cathy urged. Mrs.
Riggin finally agreed to take one magazine.

It might not be quite as easy as she had
thought, but she was making some progress.
Cathy went downstairs to get something to
eat. Mother was ironing. Chris was eating bread

and jelly. Cathy told them, chuckling, what she was doing.

Chris said plaintively, "Well, I wish, Cathy, while you're about it, you'd ask all those people if they'd like to have one of our kittens."

"O.K. I will," Cathy said agreeably.

Mother looked up, laughing. "How about selling some tickets for the church supper, dear?"

"All right," Cathy said dreamily, going upstairs with a banana.

Luck seemed to desert her now, for several calls found no one at home. Finally Cathy gave up trying to get news this afternoon. But maybe I could sell some subscriptions by telephone, she thought. That would be quicker than going out.

Suddenly she thought of old Mrs. Denny. Mrs. Denny was not on her list, because she was old and deaf and not a likely source of news. But she might like to have a good magazine to read. The more she thought about it, the more Mrs. Denny seemed like a natural prospect. If I can make her hear, Cathy thought. Maybe I ought to go down there. She decided to try by telephone first.

When Mrs. Denny answered, Cathy shouted into the phone, "This is Cathy Leonard calling. Remember?"

"Who's this?" said Mrs. Denny.

"Cathy Leonard. You know."

"I can't hear so good," said Mrs. Denny.

"Cathy Leonard! The one who writes for the *County Crier*!"

"Fire? Where's the fire?" said Mrs. Denny.

"*Crier!*" Cathy screamed. She decided quickly not to try to sell a subscription. She could never make the old lady understand. But possibly, while she was about it, she could get across something as simple as a ticket for the church supper.

"Mrs. Denny," she said, trying to speak very clearly, "I am selling tickets for the church supper. Would you like to go? They're a dollar fifty."

"What's that?" said Mrs. Denny.

"Church supper. I'm selling tickets."

"I can't hear so good," said Mrs. Denny. "Where'd you say the fire was?"

"I didn't say there was a fire." Oh dear, Cathy thought, I wish I hadn't called up! But maybe the old lady would understand something different. "Mrs. Denny, I have some lovely little kittens we would like to find a home for," she said. "Would you like to have a sweet little kitten to keep you company?"

"How much are they?" Mrs. Denny asked unexpectedly.

"Oh," Cathy said, "they're free."

"I thought you said you were selling them."

"I'm selling tickets! The kittens are free."

"Tickets are free?"

"No, kittens!"

"I can't hear so good," said Mrs. Denny. "Kittens, did you say? I thought you said tickets."

"I am selling tickets. . . ." Cathy stopped and sighed deeply; then she continued patiently. "I'm selling tickets for a church supper. They're a dollar fifty."

"Kittens are a dollar fifty?"

Suddenly, without meaning to at all, Cathy burst out laughing at the ridiculous mix-up. "Oh, Mrs. Denny," she gasped, shocked at herself, "excuse me! I'd better come down and see you. I'll come right now."

She went downstairs, still laughing. "Oh Chris," she said, wiping her eyes, "get Wiggly and come with me to see Mrs. Denny. I just

can't make her understand. . . ." She was giggling again.

"What are you laughing at? Mrs. Denny?"
Chris demanded.

"No! She's nice. I love her. I'm laughing
at how mixed up we got on the telephone."

And Mrs. Denny thought it was funny too.
She opened the door, beaming kindly upon
them. "You sure had me all mixed up. Here
I thought you were talking about tickets for
something and you were saying kittens." She
rubbed Wiggly under his chin.

The girls cast a quick look at one another
and Cathy was lost. She laughed. Her laughter was catching and Chris laughed. Mrs.
Denny chuckled in sympathy, until Cathy
could get herself under control and say, "Oh,
I was talking about tickets *and* kittens. I
brought both of them. My sister is anxious
to get rid of our three kittens. We've got the
mother, too, only she never comes into the
house, so that's all right. Wouldn't you like
Wiggly? He's awfully smart."

"His mother taught him to catch mice and
everything," Chris added. Mrs. Denny stroked
Wiggly's silken head. "And he's clean and he

isn't one bit of trouble," Chris assured her earnestly.

"He eats practically everything," Cathy put in. She made a face. "Even squash."

Mrs. Denny chuckled. "You two! Come here, cat. You want to come and live with me?" The girls held their breath. "I don't mind keeping him," the old lady said.

"Oh, thank you!" Cathy cried.

"Thank you!" Chris breathed.

"Oh, and if you would like to go to that church supper I was telling you about," Cathy added, remembering business, "the tickets are a dollar fifty. It's roast beef, and you can have seconds."

Mrs. Denny thought she would like to go to the supper, if she could get someone to take her. She bought a ticket. Cathy decided not to carry things too far by urging a magazine subscription. The girls were about to leave when the old lady said, "Where was that fire, did you say?"

"It wasn't a fire," Cathy told her. "What I said was that I was a reporter for the *Ferris County Crier*."

"Oh, you're the news girl. Well now, you

can put in the paper that my grandson and his wife are bringing their new baby to see me on Sunday."

This was an unexpected bonus. Cathy skipped home with Chris, her spirits sky-high. She could think of loads of people who might buy a ticket for the supper, and several who might possibly give a cute little kitten a home. As for the magazine subscriptions, why in the world hadn't she thought of this simple method sooner? She would get busy tomorrow.

Monday night after dinner when Cathy typed her society notes she found them rather scant. It had taken so much time to sell magazines and supper tickets and inquire about homes for cats that she had not made as many calls as usual. She had not succeeded in finding homes for Simon and Independence, but several people on her news list had bought tickets for the supper and quite a number had subscribed to magazines.

How many, she wondered? She looked down the page of society news, making a note opposite each name. *Mrs. Johnson, 3 mags. Mrs. Riggin, 1 mag. Mrs. Denny, 1 tick, one cat.* And so on. Rather good!

95

She decided to try and fill out the column by a few more calls and went upstairs to phone. But no one had any news tonight. Tomorrow she could add nothing, because Mother had shopping to do in Springdale and wanted to take her news in right after school.

From his room Jeff called sleepily for a drink of water. Oh well, this is the best I can do this time, Cathy thought. She folded the sheet of society news, then paused. What was it she had been about to do?

"Cath-y! I'm thirsty."

"I'm bringing you a drink, Jeffy." She took her news into her room, slipped it into an envelope, and then went for the water.

Mr. Stark sat at his typewriter amidst a litter of papers when she went in with her copy next day. "What have you got there?" he said, abrupt as usual, putting out his hand.

Cathy handed him the envelope. "There wasn't too much news this time, but I couldn't help it."

He glanced at the sheet. After a moment he peered closer. "What's this? 'Three mags, one mag, two ticks, one tick—one *cat*?' "

Cathy gasped. "Oh, I forgot to erase it! That was just how many magazine subscriptions I sold, and tickets for the church supper. And one lady bought—I mean took—one of our kittens. . . ."

Her voice trailed off as Mr. Stark laid the paper down, slowly and deliberately, and began to drum on his desk, gazing at her. "Do you want to be a reporter?" he inquired.

"Yes!" Cathy said, suprised at the question.

"Well, I'm sorry, but your glorious career ends right here if you pester people about buying magazines and cats."

"I am not *selling* cats," Cathy said with dignity. "I am *giving* them."

He ignored that. "People will be calling me up to complain that a kid who calls herself a reporter is pestering them to buy stuff. They'll say don't bother them any more. They'll be annoyed and cancel their subscriptions. They may even cancel their advertising. What we've got to have are *more* subscriptions and *more* advertising, not less!" He picked up Cathy's news again and waved it in front of her nose.

"I didn't think it would hurt," Cathy said miserably.

He tossed the sheet aside. "Bean supper!" He shook his head as if he still could not believe this crime had been committed.

"Roast beef," Cathy corrected softly.

He looked up at her, and for a fraction of a second something in his eyes made Cathy hope he was going to relent and forgive her. But only for a moment. "Look. After this, stick to news-getting, young lady. Or we'll forget the whole thing. Is that clear?"

"Yes," Cathy said in a low voice.

"Good-by!"

She walked out, cut to the quick. She was so subdued when she climbed into the car that Mother asked, "Everything all right?"

"Yes." She looked away. It would embarrass her to tell Mother how Mr. Stark had talked to her. She would never, never tell a soul. Her mind churned in a confusion of hurt, bewilderment, and anger.

But as usual, as they drove along, Cathy's thoughts slowly began to clear. Of one thing she was still sure—she wanted to be a reporter. If she had done something terrible, she would never do it again. (But I'm glad I've got those subscriptions, she thought with private satisfaction.) Yes, she would stick to news-getting from now on. She sighed. If only Mr. Stark wasn't always so cross!

He said he needed more subscriptions to the paper. Too bad she couldn't get some over the phone, she thought, with a momentary return of spirit. More advertising too. She probably could, if he'd let her. Miss Hobway had said something about problems Mr. Stark had had since he took over the *Crier*. People were cross sometimes when they had trouble, she reflected.

But it didn't excuse him, Cathy thought hotly, for being so disagreeable to her when she hadn't meant any harm!

One thought went through her mind, and she considered it briefly. He had not brought up the Wolf-Fox mistake of last week. That, at least, had been nice of Mr. Stark.

Mother turned into the parking space at the shopping center. "Look, Christmas trees already."

The pile of fresh evergreens was being un-loaded from a truck. Cathy sniffed the spicy fragrance as they passed, and her unquench-able spirits began to rise again. Christmas was coming. The old thrill stirred, dimming the importance of the recent unpleasantness.

She must think about presents. Chris wanted a parakeet so much—if they could get rid of the kittens. She would have to put her mind on finding homes for them. Whom did she know who might possibly be willing to take a kitten? Suddenly Cathy giggled.

"Something funny?" Mother inquired.

Cathy laughed out loud, shaking her head. "You wouldn't understand, Mother. Just something I thought of!"

She had thought of giving one of those cute kittens to cross old Mr. Stark for Christmas, to cheer him up!

Angus Answers the Phone

Suddenly Christmas lay ahead, like a galaxy of twinkling lights in the wintry distance. Cathy and Naomi began to make tiny, gay organdy aprons for presents, under Mrs. Hughes' direction.

"Cathy," Naomi said, as the two girls strolled up the drive after school, "come on in and sew."

"O.K." Cathy was trying to decide whether to put blue or lavender trim on Grandma's apron. "Oh, I can't," she remembered. "This is Tuesday."

News seemed scarce now that everyone was beginning to get ready for Christmas, and Cathy wanted to get a few more society items, if she could, before delivering her copy at six o'clock. I want it to be specially good this time, she thought, to make up for last week. She had forgiven Mr. Stark, but she intended to be careful not to incur his displeasure again.

"I'll try not to take long," she told Naomi.

Naomi sighed. "O.K., but I certainly do hate to sew all by myself!"

Cathy talked to Mother for a few minutes, then got herself an apple and started upstairs. In the upper hall there was a sudden commotion, then a gale of giggles, and Chris's bedroom door slammed shut. There was a sign on the door, *Nobody Come In*.

Cathy grinned to herself. The Christmas spirit was in the air. She felt a small surge of impatience with the dull calls she was about to make, then closed herself into Mother's room.

She called Mrs. Ferris. Nothing to report there. Mrs. Hainey was having company for dinner on Sunday. Cathy glanced down the list again, having combed it thoroughly several times. News seemed so slim that she decided to call Mrs. Mann. Perhaps Mrs.

Mann had been visiting her daughter again, and she could say, "Mrs. Oscar Mann has returned after spending. . . ." She dialed the number.

Cathy sat gazing out at the stark, gnarled trees in the orchard, the hills standing dark against the setting sun, and involuntarily she began to hum. "God rest ye merry, gentlemen." She could hear the buzz of the phone, ringing in Mrs. Mann's house. Lavender or blue? she thought. Lavender is Grandma's favorite color, but her eyes are blue. Maybe I could use both. She watched the afternoon train to New York cross the trestle at the edge of town.

Mrs. Mann was not there. What a nuisance. Cathy was lowering the receiver toward its cradle when suddenly she jumped and raised it again to her ear.

There had been a noise at the other end of the line, a clatter, as if someone had noisily removed the receiver.

"Hello?" Cathy said.

No answer. "Hello!" she repeated.

Then she heard the sound of deep barking—Angus.

Cathy listened. The barking had sounded close to the phone at first. Now it seemed to be far off, in another part of the house. "Hello!" she called. A distant, muffled bark was the only response.

Slowly Cathy hung up. That was funny, she thought. What was Angus doing, answering the phone? She sat there a moment, puzzled.

Well . . . she still needed some news. Cathy consulted her list once more and tried Mrs. Moore in Northvale. That was certainly funny about Angus answering, she thought again as she waited.

Mrs. Moore did not answer either, and suddenly Cathy decided she would not make any more phone calls now. She picked up her news items and went downstairs.

Mother was preparing vegetables for a beef stew. "Mother," Cathy said, "the funniest thing happened. A dog answered the phone."

Mother laughed. "I should think that was funny."

"Only it's queer," Cathy said. "It was Mrs. Mann's dog, Angus."

"A very smart dog, if he's trained to answer the phone. Will you please hand me the carrots, Cathy?"

Cathy got a bunch of carrots from the refrigerator. She had a thought which had not occurred to her before. "The receiver was off the hook when I hung up. I'm going to call again and see if she answers."

She went into the hall and called Mrs. Mann's number, and promptly the buzz of the busy signal responded. For a moment Cathy felt reassured. Mrs. Mann must be there now, talking to someone. But then she remembered that there would be a busy signal if the phone had been left off the hook. She went back and reported to Mother.

"Mrs. Mann is probably out, and Angus knocked the phone off the table," Mother said.

Cathy protested. "But Angus goes *everywhere* with her, Mother. She *never* leaves him home alone."

"Well, call the operator," Mother suggested. "Ask her if that line is busy or if the phone is off the hook."

Cathy called the operator. "The phone has been left off the hook," the girl reported shortly. "I am signaling."

But neither Mrs. Mann nor her dog responded to the signal.

Cathy was really curious now, curious and disturbed. "Mother, can I go down there?" she said. "There's something funny about Angus answering!"

Mother hesitated. "There's some perfectly simple explanation, I'm sure."

"But I've got such a funny feeling! Please may I go?"

"Very well. It's almost dark, so I'll go with you." Mother untied her apron, turned the vegetables into the pot of stew, and lowered the heat. "We'll take the car."

They drove down the street. Mrs. Mann's car was in her garage, but the house stood in darkness. Cathy rang the bell. Instantly the deep voice of Angus was raised inside. In a moment the big collie appeared at the window, paws on the sill. It was not an unfriendly bark, Cathy thought, but there was a note of urgency in it. Perplexed and a little frightened, she looked in at him, there in the dark house. What should she do?

And then a car turned into the drive next door, and Mr. Lindstrom got out. Oh, good, Cathy thought! "I'm going to tell Mr. Lindstrom," she called to Mother, waiting in the car, and ran down the steps and across the yard.

"She must be home," she told Mr. Lindstrom, "because her car is here and Angus is here. But her phone is off the hook, and she doesn't answer the doorbell."

Mr. Lindstrom knew that Mrs. Mann kept a key under the back mat. He went around and got it and unlocked the front door. Angus was there to meet them in a frenzy of barking.

"There, boy." Mr. Lindstrom put a hand on the dog's head. "It's all right. Quiet." He and Cathy and Mother stepped inside. Cathy's heart was pounding furiously now.

"Mrs. Mann?" Mr. Lindstrom called. They listened. He reached for the hall switch and snapped on a light.

Then they heard a response, a weak voice.

"Where are you?" Mr. Lindstrom shouted.

"Down here!"

The voice was faint, but Cathy said instantly, "In the basement."

They were in the kitchen, the light was on, and Angus was leading them to the open cellar door.

Mrs. Mann lay on the floor at the bottom of the stairs. "Thank goodness," she whispered. "My leg. I can't stand."

Mother brought a blanket and pillow, and they made her more comfortable. Mr. Lindstrom went to telephone the doctor, and Mrs. Lindstrom came over.

"I was carrying some curtains I brought home from my daughter's to wash," Mrs. Mann told them. "I fell down the whole flight. I must have fainted. I thought no one would ever. . . ." Tears of pain came to her eyes as she tried to move.

Doctor Gleason came. He examined Mrs. Mann and said she must go to the hospital for X-rays. He called an ambulance. When they had taken Mrs. Mann away, Cathy and Mother went home. The Lindstroms took Angus to their house.

"She has you and Angus to thank," Mother said. "He must have gotten excited when the phone rang." They had found the phone on the floor in the dining room. "She might have lain there all night."

"I knew it was funny!" Cathy said again and again.

She was filled with excitement at this weird adventure. As they set the table, she related the tale of the barking dog to Chris and Jeff. She went in to tell Naomi about it. Then Daddy came, and they sat down to dinner, once more going over their neighbor's misadventure.

They were eating tapioca pudding when the telephone rang. "Answer it, please, Chris," Mother said.

"It's for you, Cathy," Chris reported, coming back. "It's some man."

Cathy gave a great horrified gasp. Her copy! She had completely forgotten about getting it to the office. She sat frozen with dismay.

"Oh, Cathy, your copy!" Mother said, remembering too. "I never thought of it."

Cathy wanted to run upstairs and hide her head, go anywhere, just so she need not answer that phone and face Mr. Stark's fury. He would fire her now. She knew it. After what happened last week and the week before, this was the end.

"Go on, dear, tell him what happened," Mother said.

There was no way out. Slowly she got up from the table and went to the phone. "Hello." her voice sounded shaky with dread. "Yes, I know. I forgot."

His response was bitingly sarcastic. "Oh, you forgot!"

"Just a minute," Cathy said weakly. "I'll ask my father if he'll bring me down."

Daddy was not pleased either. "What happened?"

"It was that dog. We just forgot."

She told Mr. Stark she would have the copy there as soon as she could. "I have to type it," she added.

She wished he would fire her now and get it over with. He was going to, of course. If he would only do it now, perhaps she wouldn't have to go in and face his scorching wrath. But she ought to explain, even though she knew he would not accept any excuse. "You see, I was getting some news. I was telephoning, and this dog answered the phone, and then I thought. . . ."

"*Who* answered the phone?" the editor said.

"A dog. And I thought something must have happened, so we went down there—my mother went with me—and she was hurt, and. . . ."

"Who was hurt?" Mr. Stark demanded.

"Mrs. Mann. She fell down the cellar stairs, and she may have a broken hip. She's in the hospital now. We stayed till the ambulance came and then—well, I just forgot."

There was a long pause at the other end of the line. "Well," Mr. Stark said at last, and his voice was gruff but not furious any more, "you seem to have had a good excuse this time. O.K. Get down here as soon as you can, Cathy."

She hung up slowly. He hadn't fired her. He didn't even sound as if he was going to. That was the first time Mr. Stark ever called me by my name, Cathy thought, wonderingly. It was almost as if, for the first time, he had acknowledged her existence. She went to borrow Mrs. Hughes' typewriter.

Mr. Stark accepted her copy almost meekly. He seemed much more interested in the affair of Mrs. Mann than in any of the news she had turned in.

So another crisis was past. Mrs. Mann's hip was not broken, only deeply bruised, and she was resting comfortably in the hospital for a few days. Cathy decided to relax long enough the next afternoon to work on Christmas presents with Naomi. Besides the aprons, she was making Mother a luncheon set of soft blue cotton, finishing the edges with a stitch Mrs. Hughes had showed her.

They were discussing Christmas. "I hope I get a typewriter," Cathy remarked.

"I hope I get lots and lots of books," Naomi said.

They both wanted records and sweaters and pocketbooks. "I think I'm going to get ice skates," Naomi added, giving her mother a significant look.

There was a pounding on Naomi's door, and Chris called, "Cathy, we got the mail."

"Here's a letter for you," Jeff shouted.

"It's from the *County Crier*," Chris informed her.

Cathy slid her sewing behind a cushion on the davenport, away from Chris's eyes. Alarm leaped inside her. She was being fired after all! She had never received a letter from the paper before, so what else could it be?

Naomi opened the door and Jeff held out the letter. Cathy stared at it. "Open it," Chris said.

"I'm going upstairs to open it," said Cathy. She did not want everyone watching, if it was something bad. She went up to her room and closed the door. Then she took a letter opener from her desk and slit open the envelope.

There was only a thin pink slip inside. Slowly she drew it out, gazing at it with a puzzled frown. Then suddenly Cathy gave a shrill squeal, headed for the door, and flew downstairs, waving the paper.

"I forgot!" she cried. "I forgot all about it!"

"What?" Chris demanded.

"This is my pay! Look, Naomi!"

"Where's the money?" Jeff wanted to know.

"It's a check!" Cathy heard her mother come in the back door and rushed to the kitchen.

"How wonderful, dear." Mother paused,

her arms full of groceries, to glance at the check Cathy held before her eyes. "What are you going to do with all that money?"

"Save it. No, I'm not, I'm going to spend it!" Cathy spun about like a top. "I'm going to think of something super-super-special to spend it for, because it's the first money I ever really earned. Oh," she cried, "I'm going straight upstairs and telephone some people and earn lots more money!"

Mother laughed with her, and Cathy went off, treading air. She stopped to poke her head into Naomi's door. "Naomi, I am just going to make a couple of calls. Will you please keep my you-know-what hidden?"

All the bored feeling about her job, all the resentment of Mr. Stark's unpleasantness had fled now. The encouragement of the check had sent Cathy's spirits reaching for the stars. She simply could not wait to get started on next week's column.

"Jingle bells, jingle bells," she sang to herself, waiting with the phone at her ear and gazing out into the dusk. Beyond the village, the lights of a train went by on the trestle. "Oh, what fun it is to ride in a one-horse open—*train*," Cathy concluded unexpectedly.

The idea slid into her mind then. Mrs. Post did not answer, and Cathy hung up after a moment and sat there.

Why not spend her money on a day in New York? Bernice had seen the Christmas tree at Rockefeller Center and said it was terrific. She could take Mother and Chris and Jeff and Naomi. They could have lunch somewhere. . . .

Suddenly she was tumbling downstairs with her wonderful idea.

And Mother said they could go this Saturday. "The Christmas crowds will be horrible. But . . . it's a lovely thought, dear."

Cathy told Chris and Jeff about the treat in store and rushed in to invite Naomi. But Naomi's mother needed her that day, she said. "We have shopping to do, and I need Naomi's advice." Mother and daughter smiled at each other, and Cathy understood. Besides, Naomi had lived in New York, so going there was not such an adventure for her.

Chris and Jeff were bursting with excitement. Neither could remember ever being in New York. But Jeff was thrilled most of all at the prospect of riding on a train. He had never been on a train either.

"At least I can go to New York on a train," he said philosophically. "Because I am never, never going to get to White Plains."

It was then that Cathy had her second inspiration. "Mother," she said, when the children were discussing the great event in the other room, "why couldn't we call Grandma and ask her to meet us in New York and take Jeff back to White Plains with her for the weekend? He'd much rather do that than go shopping and all that kind of stuff with us."

They consulted Daddy. After dinner Mother called Grandma. Grandma was delighted. She would meet them at Pennsylvania Station and carry Jeff off for a gala weekend especially designed for small boys. Monday afternoon she would deliver him, by train and subway, at Daddy's office.

They told Jeff in the morning. "So you see, honey, Cathy did fix it for you," Cathy said. "I told you I would."

"Oh boy! I have to tell Mike."

Jeff's cup of joy was full. He was off, running across the road toward Mike's house, every inch of his small sturdy body fairly crackling with excitement. Cathy watched him from the door, then went to pick up her schoolbooks, still smiling.

All is Bright

The Leonards were eating dinner the next night when the doorbell rang. Cathy was getting up to go to the door when it opened and Martha put her head in.

"Hi! Can I come in?"

"Come in, Martha," Mother said. "Will you have some shortcake with us?"

"No, thank you." Martha was out of breath. "I just came over because my brother brought the *Crier* home, and I thought you'd like to see what's in it, Cathy."

"Oh, did he put in everything I sent, I wonder?" Cathy laid down her napkin and slid out of her chair.

"I don't know," Martha said, "but there's something else. Look!"

Cathy stood, the paper in her hands, gazing at the headline Martha pointed out. And as she read, she felt a blush slowly rise until both cheeks felt on fire. Her mouth opened and stayed that way until she became aware of it and closed it tightly over a pleased smile which she tried hard to suppress.

"What does it say, Cathy?" Chris asked. Cathy went on reading to herself.

"Come on, dear!" Mother urged.

Cathy did not hear. She was reading over again a headline that said: "*Crier* Correspondent goes to Aid of Injured Woman.

"Quick action of Cathy Leonard, youthful reporter to this paper," the story continued, "brought aid to an injured woman alone in her house Tuesday. Alarmed when a barking dog . . ."

Cathy read on to the end of the story, oblivious of her family. Then she looked up, the pleased smile finally breaking out. "Well! I never dreamed he'd put it in the paper!"

"Put what in the paper?" Chris demanded.

Suddenly Cathy was embarrassed by her new-found fame. "You tell them," she said to Mother, giving her the paper. She ran into the kitchen and, safely out of sight, sat down and hid her face on her knees. Here she could hear the family's reaction without letting them see her.

Mother read the story aloud. "I'll be dog-goned," said Daddy.

Chris said, "Cathy was nice to go over there. Cathy is famous now, Jeffy, because her name's in the paper."

"Isn't that just wonderful?" said Martha, proud of her friend. "You can keep the paper. 'By, Cathy!" she called.

" 'By. Thank you!" Cathy called back. But she stayed in the kitchen, glad of the excuse to start scraping the dishes. She was not ac-customed to such prominence, and it was un-comfortable.

Mother brought the dessert plates out. "That was a nice story," she said matter-of-factly.

"I guess so," Cathy replied. She was re-lieved that Mother treated the thing lightly.

Of course, though, she thought later, it really was nice of Mr. Stark to write that story, when he had been so cross with her for forgetting to take in the news.

She faced going to school with a kind of dread. Bernice and Gloria would be jealous, and everybody would look at her curiously, and she would blush. She did not quite know how to act.

Waiting for the bus next morning, Naomi and Martha and Gretchen talked about the story. "I was so excited when I read it!" Gretchen exclaimed. "My father says you're very smart, Cathy."

"Of course she is," Naomi said loyally.

"Oh!" Cathy tried not to show how flattered she felt. "It wasn't anything."

The bus came and they climbed on. Several girls in the front hailed her. "Cathy, we read in the paper about you!"

"Sit with me, Cathy!"

One of the boys in her class leaned forward. "Bowwow! Hey, Cathy, I'm injured. Save me!"

Everyone giggled, and suddenly Cathy felt

better. This kind of banter she knew how to handle. Flushed and happy, she flapped her hand at her teaser. "Oh, be quiet!"

She was a heroine. Everyone wanted to be her friend, even Bernice. As Cathy got off the bus Bernice caught up with her. "Cathy, do you want to know about my mother and father going to another convention? I mean my mother's going too, so could you put that in the paper?"

"Uh—sure," Cathy said. She was not quite prepared for this show of warmth.

"I wrote down the place." Bernice had the information to hand her.

Gloria was beside her too. "I might have some news next week, Cathy."

As they went into school Martha whispered, "They want to be on your side now, because your name was in the paper."

"Well," Cathy said, "I don't care what side they're on if they just give me some news."

There was one note this morning that was not sweet. Miss Riker congratulated Cathy on the story about her. Then she said, "Being a reporter is fine, Cathy, and being a heroine is fine too. But you used to get a hundred every day in arithmetic, and now you regularly miss one or two problems. Your other work has slipped too. What are we going to do about this?"

Cathy was in too much of a whirl this morning to be discouraged. "I promise I'll get a hundred every day from now on," she assured her teacher.

But the day passed in a kind of rosy dream, and she hardly knew what she was doing. It was almost dismissal time when Mrs. Breck, from Mr. Moore's office, came in with a note for Miss Riker. The teacher read it, glancing in Cathy's direction. "Cathy, will you go to the office, please?"

Cathy's brow wrinkled in perplexity. Obediently she accompanied Mrs. Breck down the hall.

"Why do I have to go to the office?"

"You'll see. Go right in, Cathy."

There was a man with the principal. Cathy had never seen him before. She looked uncertainly at Mr. Moore.

"Hello, Cathy," Mr. Moore said. "Sit down.

This gentleman is a reporter from the *New York World*—Mr. Hicks. He'd like to talk to you."

"To me?"

"Suppose I leave you two alone," Mr. Moore said jovially, and departed.

Cathy felt completely mystified. She looked at Mr. Hicks from the *New York World*, and he smiled at her disarmingly. "I'd just like to ask you a few questions, Cathy." He pulled a paper from his pocket, and she saw that it was a copy of the *Crier*. "I happen to live in Springdale, and I saw this story about you last night. It's rather unusual, a girl of your age being a reporter. Just how old are you?"

"Ten and a half," Cathy said.

"How did you happen to become a reporter?"

She told him about Miss Hobway. "She used to call up sometimes to see if we—my mother, that is—had any news for the society column. So sometimes, when I heard about some news, I used to call her up. And then she wanted to go to Florida, only she had to get somebody to send in the news, and she couldn't find anyone in Middle Bridge or Northvale to do it. So she thought maybe I'd like to, if my mother helped me, and she asked me."

"And do you like being a reporter?"

"Oh yes!"

"You don't have any trouble getting news, or writing it?"

"Not getting it."

"Writing it?"

"Well, my mother has to type it over sometimes." She grinned at him, relaxing.

Mr. Hicks asked about her family and what they thought of her being a reporter.

"My brother and sister—well, especially my brother—he's only six—think I ought to play with them more."

"And your mother and father?"

"My mother doesn't mind. At first my father didn't like me to use the telephone so much, but now he's used to it."

"Now about this"—he glanced at the paper in his hand—"Mrs. Mann. Tell me about that."

She was glad to. Mr. Hicks proved a flattering audience, and Cathy was startled, when she happened to glance out the window, to see that the buses were loading. She had not heard the dismissal bell.

"Oh, I've got to go or I'll miss the bus!"

He stood up at once. "O.K., Cathy. Thank you very much."

She hesitated. "Why did you ask me all those questions?"

"I like to talk to a fellow reporter." He grinned at her. "So long, Cathy. Good luck."

The girls were holding a seat. "Why did you have to go to the office, Cathy?" Naomi asked.

"Some man wanted to talk to me."

"What about?"

"That story in the paper." Cathy was still uncomfortable about her fame. She didn't want to discuss it any more with the girls. "Oh!" She gazed out the window and dismissed the subject. "I hope it's a day like this when we go to New York tomorrow!"

She mentioned the interview to Mother. "Is he writing a story about you for the *World?*" Mother asked.

"Oh no!" Cathy was shocked at the idea. "He just said he liked to talk" . . . she felt a pleased blush mounting . . . "to a fellow reporter."

Saturday was exactly the day for a Christmas-shopping expedition. Cathy was up in the frosty dawn. Her best tweed coat, with cap to match, was laid out, with shoulder bag and white gloves. Chris's outfit was similar, but blue instead of brown. Jeff looked scrubbed and pink in his Sunday suit, and Mother was just beautiful, Cathy thought.

Daddy took them to Princeton Junction. The day was cold, with a great blustery wind blowing and a glorious blue-and-gold sky, and there was frost on the windows of the warm, sunny railroad coach.

They turned a seat over and sat cozily face to face. Jeff gazed out, spellbound, as farms, towns hung with Christmas lights, and then the Jersey meadows sped by, giving way finally to the grimy factories on the outskirts of the city and at last the tunnel.

Cathy sat next to Jeff, tightly holding her purse with the money in it. She caught Mother's glance.

"You should see your face, Cathy."

"Is it dirty?" Cathy asked in alarm.

"No, it's happy!"

In Pennsylvania Station, which was big and cavernous and smelled of fruit stands and smoke, they saw Grandma coming toward them, smiling. She enveloped them all in hugs. "Jeffy, are you coming with me for a lovely visit?" He nodded. "Know what we're going to do today, you and I?" His eyes were on her, wondering, trusting. "We're going to the museum. Then we're going to have a lovely lunch, and we're going to ride on a train to White Plains. And tomorrow—well, I know where there's a park, with bears."

Jeff's hand slipped into Grandma's. He was ready. " 'By, dear," Mother said lightly. "Have a good time."

Cathy and Chris hugged him and looked after his small departing back. When they turned away Cathy felt as if she had lost something she always carried, and she slipped her hand into Mother's.

Chris said, "I wish Jeff was coming with us!"

"Now!" Mother changed the subject briskly. "Shall we get a taxi or find a bus?"

"Bus!"

Out in the noisy, windy, thrilling city they rode to Fifth Avenue and got off to stroll north. There were such crowds it was almost impossible for three to walk together. In front of a big store people stood in great huddles to see the windows, and after a while Cathy and Chris managed to get close enough to see the display of fairy-tale characters in bewitching costumes.

Carols drifted through the air from an unseen source, and lights sprayed across the front of a building in the shape of a dazzling Christmas tree. There were more windows with Christmas gifts spilled about, mingled with twinkling tinsel and richly hued ornaments.

Then they were at Rockefeller Center with its great tree, colored balls bobbing in the wind, and they were gazing down at the skating rink that breathed icy air on the onlookers lining the rail above. There was music here, too, and the bright costumes of the skaters made an endlessly shifting pattern.

"Cold?" Mother asked.

Not Cathy. She felt glowing and warm and thrilled. But Chris was cold. So they walked on and came to a church, and went in out of the cutting wind. Far away, in the front of the church, a choir was rehearsing Christmas music.

Cathy sat rapt. She had never been in a great church like this. Mother pointed out the deep-blue stained-glass windows and the tall columns soaring into the vaulted ceiling.

Then they went out again, and Cathy was suddenly starving. "Where are you taking us for lunch, dear?" Mother asked, her eyes twinkling down at her daughter.

"I don't know," Cathy admitted with a chuckle. "You're invited, but I don't know where."

Mother suggested a Swedish restaurant nearby. It was quite elegant, Cathy thought. A waiter settled them at a table and brought crisp rolls and wonderful dark bread and sweet butter and a tray of icy olives and celery.

"This is a smorgasbord," Mother explained. "We go up to that table and help ourselves."

Cathy was astonished to see that the serving table revolved slowly before them. Everything moved around—many varieties of fish, handsome molded salads, cold meats, chicken and ham, baked beans and pickles, and tiny hot dogs and cheeses, in glorious, delicious profusion. Cathy let it all go by once, trying to make up her mind, but the second time the table came by she was ready, quickly filling her plate as the delicacies moved along.

Chris needed help. She gave soft little moans as the food escaped while she was making up her mind. Cathy and Mother came to her assistance.

They went back a second time. Cathy liked everything except one kind of cheese, which Chris said looked like soap.

"Tastes like soap, too!" Cathy said, making a face.

The restaurant filled. Waiters moved deftly about. Soft music played, and a lighted Christmas tree, gay with ornaments and lights, brightened the dimly lit room. Oh, I could stay here forever, Cathy thought.

Then came the supreme moment when she laid her money on a silver tray and the waiter bowed and carried it off. This moment was worth all the hours of tiresome telephoning, all the unpleasantness she had endured at the hands of Mr. Stark.

"Thank you, dear," Mother was saying. "This was a lovely treat."

"Thank you, Cathy," Chris echoed. "Mother, could I be a reporter when I get big, like Cathy?"

Cathy sat straight, and over Chris's earnest head she smiled at Mother. This, too, was her reward.

They spent a lovely afternoon wandering and looking and shopping just a bit in the crowded stores. Then it was time to go home. Chris wanted to buy candy to take to Jeff, and suddenly they realized that Jeff would not be there. It was hard to picture home without him. They bought the candy for Daddy.

There was a wait for their train, and Mother bought a paper to read. Chris wandered, exploring the station waiting room, but Cathy sat beside her mother on the bench, reliving every moment of the day.

Suddenly Mother exclaimed, "Cathy!"

Cathy jumped. "What?"

"Here's a story about you!"

The paper was the *World,* and in the *World* was everything she had told Mr. Hicks. Even about—oh dear, she shouldn't have said that, Cathy saw now—about Daddy not wanting her to be on the phone so much! "But—he didn't tell me he was going to write anything!" she kept repeating as she read.

She felt quite overcome. Two newspaper stories about her! Cathy was in a daze when they got on the train. Chris, on the other hand, took the story calmly. She knew Cathy was famous now, so why get excited over one more story?

Daddy read the article and looked at Cathy reflectively, a smile playing about his mouth. "Well, toots, you're really knocking them over." He was pleased, Cathy could tell.

She could not eat supper. She went in to show the story to Naomi and then, suddenly tired of the whole thing, launched with relief into an account of their day.

"And then we had lunch at this adorable place. . . ." Telling Naomi about it was almost as much fun as the day itself.

"I'm going to New York soon," Naomi

said. "We know some people, the Master-sons, who are going to Europe, and when they get to New York my mother and I are going in to see them. We're going to stay all night with my aunt."

Before bedtime Mrs. Stark phoned. This time Cathy was not afraid of him. "Have you seen tonight's *New York World*?" he asked.

"Yes."

"Oh. Well, I just wanted to let you know about it."

Mother smiled when Cathy repeated the brief conversation. "I think you've become an asset to Mr. Stark," she said.

"What's an asset?"

"Something valuable."

"Why am I valuable to him?"

"When people read this story about you in the *World,* they read about the *County Crier* too, you see. That's good for Mr. Stark's business. Incidentally, Mrs. Gray told me she hadn't taken the *Crier* for a long time, there was so little Middle Bridge news, but since you've been calling her up she has subscribed again."

"That's good," Cathy said. "Mr. Stark said he needed more subscriptions."

Monday morning at breakfast she said, "Oh, I hope none of the kids at school read that story!"

"Why?" Mother asked.

"They'll tease me again."

But deep in her heart Cathy really hoped everyone had seen the story. Fame was sweet, especially among her own schoolmates.

And she really was famous again. She knew that instantly when she climbed on the bus trying to look unaware. Bernice and Gloria were obviously so impressed that they did not know what to say to her. There was more teasing and banter from the boys, and Cathy blushed and giggled.

Oh, it was fun to be so important! She had seemed a little important when she could ask her classmates to give her news, and even more important when the *Crier* printed that story. But now—well, Cathy felt that she had reached a pinnacle of fame never achieved before, at least in the River View School.

True, Miss Riker merely looked at her with

a small, doubtful smile. But Mr. Moore, Mrs. Breck and Mr. Lippo all congratulated her warmly.

Monday afternoon Cathy and Chris were watching the window long before Daddy's bus was due. They set the table early to kill time. At last the bus drew up, its lights cheery in the twilight. "Here they are!" Chris cried, and was out the door.

Jeff was running up the drive. He could not wait to get his coat off before telling his news. "We saw a dinosaur. He was dead. And stars that moved in a pretend sky. And some bears. . . ."

Suddenly home seemed right once more. Cathy went humming into the kitchen.

When she went to bed that night Jeff called from his room. "Cathy, I want a drink of water." She took it to him, and he sat up and drank. "Cathy."

"Yes." She sat down on the edge of the bed.

"I'm going to help you get news."

"You are?"

"Yes, every day."

136

"Thank you, Jeffy."

It was not because she was famous; Jeff did not know about that. And probably he had forgotten that Cathy had been responsible for his getting to White Plains—Cathy had almost forgotten it herself. Jeffy only knew that tonight he felt warm and loving toward his big sister.

It was a nice feeling to have Jeff want to help her. He had been so cross about all the time she spent on her job. Chris had been sweet, except for a little grumbling about dishes. And Daddy hadn't said much lately. Besides, he had really been pleased, she thought, about those two newspaper stories.

Cathy got ready for bed in a state of dreamy contentment. Just before she drifted off, the words of a Christmas carol floated across her mind. "All is calm, all is bright." Eyes closed, she tried to sing them softly to herself to express the way she felt. "All is bright." But she was too deliciously sleepy.

Weekend

"But we'd have to spend the night," Mother said.

Cousin Dick Godfrey and his wife were to be in New York, and they were having dinner at Great-aunt Jessie's the Saturday before Christmas. Grandma was anxious to have Daddy and Mother come too.

"What if we do spend the night?" said Daddy. "We haven't seen Dick and Laura for ten years. The children will be all right. Mrs. Hughes is here." So at last Mother agreed to go.

"Good," Cathy said with satisfaction. "That's one news item. 'Mr. and Mrs. Philip Leonard were guests. . . .' "

138

"That's all you think about," Chris told her mildly, shaking her head.

Friday afternoon Cathy and Naomi came home to find Mother and Mrs. Hughes talking. Mother said "Hello, dear," but she seemed distracted and so did Mrs. Hughes.

"What's the matter?" Cathy asked, and Naomi looked at her mother questioningly.

"We've run into a little problem," said Mother.

"It's our friends the Mastersons," Mrs. Hughes told Naomi. "They *would* take this weekend, of all times, to arrive in New York. Aunt Eva called and said she expected us tomorrow to spend the night."

"Oh, may we stay alone?" Cathy asked Mother quickly.

"Indeed you may not," Mother said. "But I talked to Daddy on the phone and he still wants to go. I think I have a woman to stay with you."

"Who?"

"A Mrs. March. She lives in Springdale. She's a practical nurse, and she's used to children."

"I feel awful about this," Mrs. Hughes said.

"It isn't your fault," Mother told her. "By the way, Cathy," she added, "there was a phone call for you. Someone has some news. Here's the number."

"Oh, good." Cathy gazed at the number, pleased. Quite a few people had called up to give her news during the week. It was wonderful that news was actually coming to her now. Those stories in the *Crier* and the *World* seemed to have awakened people to the fact that Cathy Leonard really was a reporter.

She had looked forward to being head of the Leonard household while her parents were away, even though Mrs. Hughes would be there if needed. She and Naomi had made their plans to have meals together and to work on all sorts of Christmas projects. This new development was a disappointment to both of them.

However, Cathy thought, the weekend would be a novelty. Mother and Daddy had never been away overnight before. She was relieved when Mother talked to Mrs. March again that night and the arrangement became definite.

"She can't get here before four-thirty,"

Mother told them. "We'll have to leave by three. Will you all be sure to stay right here until Mrs. March comes?"

Chris and Jeff promised.

"I'll be busy phoning," Cathy said.

"But you keep an eye on your brother and sister," Daddy instructed her.

Mother asked what they would like to have to eat while she was away.

"Hamburger," said Jeff.

"Jello with stuff in it," Chris said.

"Mashed potatoes," said Jeff.

"Olives. A big bottle," Cathy ordered.

The three stood in the drive, waving their mother and father away Saturday afternoon. It was a strange feeling to see the car carrying both their parents disappear around the bend in the road. Mrs. Hughes and Naomi had left for New York that morning.

The house seemed strangely empty and silent as Cathy went back indoors. But she had a pleasant sense of being monarch of all she surveyed. She was head of the family now, and she relished it. "Remember, don't go out of the yard, children," she called in her most grown-up tone before she climbed the stairs.

141

Saturday was often a good day for her telephoning. Cathy made three calls and obtained a news item from each call. Before she could pick up the phone a fourth time it rang, and a woman on the outskirts of town told her about an arriving guest.

Chris came upstairs. "I feel lonely. What can I do, Cathy?"

"Why don't you play with Jeff?" Cathy was busy making notes and did not look up.

"He's up in the tree."

"Well, why don't you go up there with him?"

Chris lingered a moment, then wandered away, and Cathy turned back to the telephone hardly aware that her sister had been there and departed.

It was some time later that she heard the front door open and the sound of loud weeping. Cathy put the receiver in its cradle and went out in the hall. Chris and Jeff were climbing the stairs and Chris was uttering consoling sounds.

"What happened?" Cathy called.

"Jeffy fell out of the tree."

"Oh, Jeffy, come here!" Cathy held out

her arms and Jeff walked into them, tear-stained and grieving. "How far did you fall?"

"Four miles!"

Obviously he was not gravely injured. "Where did you hurt yourself?" Cathy asked.

"Here." He patted his solid little rear.

"Oh, too bad!" Cathy rubbed tenderly, and Jeff's cries of pain subsided to pitiful sniffs. The telephone rang.

"Don't telephone any more!" Jeff threw his arms around her, with fresh wails.

"Jeffy, I have to just answer. I won't be two seconds."

But it was more news, and it took longer than that. Her attention only half on the phone call, Cathy watched the two go off, Chris's arm protectingly around Jeff.

As soon as she could she went downstairs. The children were doing jigsaw puzzles on the floor and scarcely looked up. Chris, not she, had been Jeff's solace in distress.

"It's dark here," Cathy said. "And it's cold." She snapped on lights and turned up the thermostat, hearing the comforting thud of the oil burner going on. Her eyes fell on the clock. "It's after five o'clock. Where's that

Mrs. March? Well, she'll be here any minute now," she went on cheerfully. "I'm going to start dinner."

The telephone rang. "Oh, bother," Cathy said, and went to answer it in the hall.

But this time it was Mother's voice. "Hello, dear. We just got here. Everything all right?"

"Oh yes, it's fine," Cathy told her.

"That's good. Let me speak to Mrs. March."

The children had scrambled up and were clamoring. "Chris and Jeff want to speak to you," Cathy said.

"When are you coming home?" Chris cried into the phone.

"I fell out of the tree!" Jeff shouted.

"Oh, be quiet, Jeff. He didn't hurt himself," Cathy assured her mother hastily.

"Well, I'm certainly glad of that! Now may I talk to Mrs. March, Cathy?"

Cathy hesitated. "She isn't—exactly—here," she said finally.

"Not there! Hasn't she come?"

"Not yet."

There was a conference at the other end, and Daddy came on the phone. "Haven't you heard from Mrs. March?"

"No."

"Give me her number. It's in the little book."

She read him the number and he said, "I'll call her, and then I'll call you right back. Are you sure you're all right? Jeff wasn't hurt?"

"No, he's fine."

"Well, keep your eye on him."

This was a situation, Cathy thought, hanging up. At least she could enjoy being in charge a little while longer. She bustled into the kitchen to start dinner before the sitter arrived to take over or some other unforeseen development occurred.

Mother had left everything in readiness. Cathy snapped on burners. Hamburgers were sizzling, potatoes bubbling, and she was stirring the succotash when Daddy called again.

"Mrs. March was taken suddenly sick," he said. "She's had somebody trying to get you since three o'clock."

"We were right here!" Cathy said indignantly.

"Your line was busy."

She gave a small gasp of realization. Of course. She had been on the phone herself.

"Look," Daddy said, "what about your dinner?"

"It's almost ready."

"Eat it. We're coming home. We'll be there around midnight."

"Oh!" Cathy gave a loud wail. "Daddy, *please* don't come home!"

She was dismayed. Not only could she not bear to have this novel experience end so soon, but she remembered how Daddy, especially, had looked forward to the little outing. How awful that he and Mother had to come all the way home tonight!

Then she thought of something else. "I've got it written for the paper!" she cried.

"That's just too bad," Daddy retorted. "Cathy, if anything comes up, call Mrs. McArdle. We'll get there as soon as we can after we have our dinner. Have Chris and Jeff go to bed, but you may wait up for us if you want to."

She hung up, miserable. Chris and Jeff stood at her elbow. "Are they coming home?" Chris asked.

"I guess so."

"Good!" Chris said.

"Good!" Jeff echoed, nodding his approval.

Cathy looked at her brother and sister, and the thought went through her mind that she should have played with them this afternoon and made it fun, instead of telephoning all that time. They're not used to being here without Mother and Daddy, she thought. They're not having a good time. And now Mother and Daddy's fun is spoiled. . . .

Suddenly she jumped up from the telephone table with fierce resolve and marched purposefully toward the kitchen. The children trailed after her, sensing action. "What are you going to do, Cathy?" Chris asked.

"I am going to turn off the stove first," Cathy said. "Everything's done." She turned off the burners. "Now I am going to find somebody to come here and stay all night, so Mother and Daddy can stay at Grandma's!"

"How will you find someone?" Jeff's eagerness to have his mother and father home was sidetracked as Cathy's plan caught his interest.

"I know where practically everybody in Middle Bridge is this minute. I know who's gone away and who's home, and I'll just call till I find *somebody* who can come. I'll go get my list of names."

She went down the familiar list, Chris and Jeffy pressing against her. She paused at each name of someone near at hand. Most women had families. Some had company or were away this evening. Mrs. Lindstrom was home, she knew, but she wouldn't want to leave Mr. Lindstrom. Mrs. Stewart and Mrs. Denny were too old.

"Cathy," Chris said, "that lady you rescued."

"I was just thinking of her," Cathy said. "She didn't go to her daughter's, because her leg still hurts a little. But she can walk all right. She can even drive the car. I'm going to call her."

Mrs. Mann not only was home, but she would be delighted to come and spend the night with them. She had finished her dinner. When she heard the story she said that she would be there, in fact, in fifteen minutes.

"She's going to bring Angus, too," Cathy announced triumphantly to the expectant children as she hung up.

"Oh, oh, oh, oh!" Chris sang, spinning around. "We're going to have fun with Angus!"

"Whoopee!" Jeff shouted.

"I'll wait till she gets here before I call Mother and Daddy," Cathy decided.

She was filled with elation as she mashed the potatoes in the electric mixer, dumping in milk and butter with a lavish hand. Chris and Jeff weren't going to have a gloomy, lonely evening after all. And she could hardly wait to tell Mother and Daddy they could relax, stop worrying about their deserted children, and have a good time with Cousin Dick and Laura.

Chris was happily shaking olives into a dish, stopping to sample a few. Jeff was vigorously pouring milk and spilling some. Cathy carried the platter of meat and the vegetable dishes to the dining table.

"Dinner is served!" she announced. They sat down to the overdone meal with ravenous appetites.

Mrs. Mann and Angus arrived before they reached the jello, and the children were setting up the card table for a game of old maid when Cathy made her call.

She talked to Mother. Mother talked to Mrs. Mann. Then Daddy wanted to speak to Cathy again. "Well, toots, you saved the day. Everything all right now?"

"It always was all right," Cathy retorted. "Only you wouldn't believe me!"

She could hear him chuckle. "You old— reporter!" Daddy said.

The children wanted to talk to their parents again. Jeff said, "Angus is going to sleep on my bed, Daddy." Chris kissed the air with a smack that went all the way to White Plains.

Then they all said together into the phone, "Good night!"

Cathy Decides

It was the Mondy before Christmas. Christmas came on Friday this year, so there was half a week of school before the holidays began. As Cathy slipped into her coat and gathered her books after breakfast she should have been atingle with anticipation. The class was going to decorate the room today. There would be a lighted Christmas tree in the school foyer, a whiff of balsam in every corridor, and the burst of carols through opened doors.

Mother and Daddy had brought Grandma home for the holidays—Grandma and a pile of beautifully wrapped presents, now reposing in Grandma's closet. Cathy had tiptoed in and peeked, just to allow herself the exquisite pleasure of dwelling upon which ones might be for her. She rather favored the large box wrapped in midnight blue and silver stars and the small fat package in plain gold paper.

But this morning all the Yuletide joy could not lift Cathy's spirits. She did not know what was wrong—she just felt subdued and a little depressed.

Naomi chattered about her weekend in New York as they headed for the bus. "But, Cathy," she said, "wasn't it exciting when the sitter didn't come and you got dinner all alone and everything?"

Something winced inside Cathy, as if Naomi had touched the source of her trouble this morning. It had to do with the weekend. Whatever it was, she edged away from something she did not want to think about.

"Yes, it was very exciting," she said quickly. "What else did you do in New York?"

But as she climbed onto the school bus, in a flash of enlightenment Cathy knew what had been worrying her. Naomi had given her the clue. It was Chris and Jeff. What she saw now, as if it would haunt her forever, was the pair of them turning away from her Saturday afternoon, Jeff in tears, Chris consoling.

Why did it bother her so much? They had all had a marvelously good time with Mrs. Mann and Angus. But somehow Cathy had the feeling that she had skirted—not entirely escaped, in fact—a great danger. It was not Jeff's falling out of a tree that bothered her. Jeff might have fallen out of a tree when Mother was home. But she was the big sister to whom they had turned when Mother and Daddy left them. And that old telephoning had taken all her attention when they needed cheer and comfort. She had let them go down alone, Jeff weeping, into a dark, chilly house. . . .

Thinking her thoughts, surrounded by the babble of her schoolmates, Cathy was alarmed and embarrassed to find actual tears stinging her eyes.

"Are you *crying,* Cathy?" Martha asked, glancing at her in astonishment.

"Of course not! It's just a little cold." She shook out her clean handkerchief with a flourish.

What an old silly I am, she thought impatiently. I start crying at the goofiest things. I'm just crazy, and I'm not going to think about it any more!

She could not, nevertheless, think herself into a mood of gaiety. Cathy practically never felt like this; but today she was quivery all over, almost waiting for some blow that was bound to fall. So she was scarcely surprised when Miss Riker said, "Cathy, will you wait a moment before you go to lunch? I would like to speak to you."

The class, chattering, filed out into the corridor through the door, which was hung with pine boughs and golden bells. When they were all gone the teacher said, "Sit down there at the front desk, Cathy."

Miss Riker sat at her own desk and glanced down at some papers before her. She looked at Cathy. "You know you have been one of my best students, probably the top pupil in this class."

Cathy gazed at her teacher. She took her high standing for granted.

"But, Cathy, for the first time I cannot give you straight A grades on your progress report. In fact," Miss Riker said reluctantly, "I am not sure I can even give you a B in arithmetic."

Cathy gave a small gasp of dismay. This she had not expected. "But—I haven't made so many mistakes!"

"Far too many for you. You can do, and you always have done, so much better. This job, Cathy." Miss Riker regarded her soberly. "It's too much for you to handle with your school work."

"Oh, Miss Riker. . . ."

"I know. You enjoy it. But it's very unusual for a child of your age to have such a job."

Cathy was eager to explain. "You see, it was very hard at first, but now it's much, much easier. Because the kids in school help me lots, and people call me up, and my father—well, he didn't exactly approve, because I was always telephoning and everything, but now he's used to it. And Mr. Stark—he's the editor—he didn't even think I could do it, and he didn't like me much. But now he does— I *think* he does. Everything's fine now!"

How could she convince Miss Riker?

"Could I still get A's if I got everything perfect from now on?" she asked. The drop in grades did bother her—more than she was willing to admit even to herself.

Miss Riker said slowly. "You are doing very indifferent work. Aren't good marks important to you any more, Cathy?"

"Oh yes!" Cathy gasped.

"Does being a reporter mean so much?"

Cathy could not put into words the reasons why it did mean so much. There was the satisfaction of tracking down news—and seeing it in print, especially when Mr. Stark had thought she couldn't do it. There was the exalted position she held among her classmates—so much more exalted, of course, since the newspapers had spread abroad her name and the distinction of being a reporter at the age of ten and a half. How could she give up this glory? Last, but really least, in spite of the wonderful day in New York, was the delightful thought that once a month that check would come along.

"You must spend hours on it," Miss Riker said.

"Well, quite a few." She could not explain,

either, that the hours meant nothing, compared with the satisfaction the work gave her.

"I don't know what more I can say," the teacher told her.

"Miss Riker," Cathy said impulsively, "honest and truly, I'll be much, much more careful with homework!"

"Well, go and have your lunch now."

But Cathy, as she joined Naomi and Martha, was more troubled than she had admitted to her teacher. Even though the work was going more smoothly, it still took many hours. It still had to be done in the afternoons. She had to help set the table or dry dishes, and do homework at bedtime. It was the same old circle. There wasn't any answer.

Unless, of course, she just gave up the job. I can't *bear* to give it up, Cathy thought fiercely.

I can't bear to get a C, either, she thought quickly. She had never had a C in her life. The very idea seemed like a nightmare.

She had been troubled when she left for school that morning; she was deeply disturbed when she got home.

Mother and Grandma were having a cup of tea. Mother looked at her keenly. "Did you have a good day, dear? Would you like some cinnamon toast and a glass of milk?"

"No, thank you. I'm not hungry. I'm going up to telephone." The habit was so strong that even today she could not break it.

She had reached the top step when she suddenly paused, because down below she had heard Grandma say, "Doesn't Cathy ever just play? All I've ever seen that child do is to plug away at that newspaper work. She doesn't look well."

Cathy could not hear Mother's low reply. After a moment she tiptoed into her room and closed the door softly.

Well, Grandma was right; she didn't have time to play. But right now—well, tomorrow was Tuesday again, time to get her news in. Cathy listlessly took her list of names and her pad and pencil from her desk. Her eyes fell on a pile of Christmas wrappings, untouched. When was she going to find time to begin wrapping presents?

Suddenly Cathy threw herself down on her bed and closed her eyes. She wished she could forget the whole thing. Around whirled her mind like a merry-go-round. Homework—C grades—"Doesn't that child ever play? She doesn't look well."—unwrapped Christmas presents—Chris and Jeff. Yes, Chris and Jeff. . . .

She opened her eyes. It was pitch-dark in her room. Cathy sat up, pushed off the warm afghan someone had thrown over her, and rubbed her eyes. Then she saw that the illuminated hands of her little clock pointed to six. She had been asleep for two hours! She slid off the bed and went down to the kitchen, blinking in the light. Dinner appeared to be almost ready.

"Did you have a lovely nap, dear?" Mother said. "I peeked in at you. I tried to keep the children quiet."

"Cathy!" Jeff cried. "Grandma is going to take Simon home to live with her! She promised. Mother, Cathy's awake, so now can I sing Grandma the song our class learned?"

"Cathy." Chris came in trailing paper and ribbon. "Would you have any time to help me wrap something up?"

"I—all right." She had wasted the whole afternoon, but there wasn't time to make any calls before dinner, Cathy decided, and anyhow, she wasn't going to brush Chris aside again.

At dinner Daddy said, "By the way, Cathy, I meant to tell you I met Joe Riggin. They're going to Florida. I jotted down the date. You can use that for a big news item." He passed her a slip of paper.

"Oh, thank you, Daddy."

As they got up from the table Mother said, "Grandma will dry the dishes. Go on and get your work done, Cathy."

Usually she was delighted to be relieved of household tasks. Tonight she felt reluctant. She wanted to be part of this family. "I'll clear the table," she said.

Jeff opened the back door and a rush of cold air swooped in. "Brr! Close that door, Jeff!" Mother cried.

"I wanted to smell the Christmas tree."

The tree stood on the back porch, big and fragrant and icy cold, ready to be brought in and decorated on Christmas Eve.

"Daddy and Jeff and me—I—are going to get the ornaments down," Chris was saying.

"Grandma, I'll tell you a secret if you cross your heart not to tell!" Jeff shouted.

They were all doing things without her, taking it for granted she did not wish to be included. Cathy went slowly upstairs. She was behind in her telephoning and her homework was untouched, but it was hard to think about doing either. She stood in the door of her room, looking from her newspaper notes on the bed to the desk where her schoolbooks lay. At last Cathy walked slowly over to her desk, sat down, and opened her arithmetic.

She slept restlessly that night. She dreamed she was trying to reach a bird with an A on its head that flapped its wings and flew off to Florida. Mother and Daddy and Chris and Jeff kept turning their backs and going away too, although she called to them, and she was left with Mr. Stark, who pounded his fist on the *County Crier* and showed his teeth like a wolf.

Sometime in the night she woke up. Her mind felt clear, and lying there in the dark she knew, quite calmly, what she was going to do. She was going to give up her work for the *County Crier*.

Only, when she thought of losing her lofty position at school, of no longer being that

living marvel, the ten-and-a-half-year-old reporter, she felt as if she could not bear it.
She pulled the covers over her head and cried
a little.

Then, seeking the comfort of human company, she got out of bed and pattered into
Chris's room. "Move over, Chris," she whispered.

Chris murmured in her sleep and moved
over. Cathy snuggled up to her back.

In the morning Chris was gazing at Cathy
when the latter opened her eyes. "Why are
you in bed with me?"

"Because I'm going to stop working for
the *County Crier*. And I felt lonely."

"Honest, are you going to stop?" Chris sat
up, wide-eyed with delight.

"Why should you care?" Cathy asked.

"Because you won't have to telephone all
the time. And you can play with me and Jeff!
I'm going to tell Jeffy!" Chris scrambled out
of bed.

"Silly," Cathy said. But she lay there, pon-
dering Chris's excitement.

Since she had made up her mind she had

had another idea. On her way to breakfast she stopped at Naomi's door.

"Mrs. Hughes, I decided something," she said. "I'm not going to work for the *County Crier* any more."

"Cathy!" Naomi gasped. "Honest?"

Again Cathy was taken aback. "But," she went on after a moment, "I don't like to—you know—let Mr. Stark down, because I promised Miss Hobway. So I wondered—would you have any time to send in news, Mrs. Hughes? I mean, if he can't get somebody right away—because you're an author. . . ."

"I think I could," Mrs. Hughes said. "For a while. Miss Hobway will be back in a couple of months, won't she?"

So that was settled. Beginning to feel better or, at least, reconciled to her decision, Cathy slipped into her place at the breakfast table. "I have an announcement to make," she said to Mother and Grandma. "I am going to stop working for the *Crier.*"

Mother looked up quickly.

"Good!" said Grandma.

"Honey, I'm glad you are!" Mother told her warmly.

No one asked why. Apparently everyone was too pleased to raise any questions.

Now there remained the task of telling her schoolmates. That was not going to be easy. Give up a wonderful job that made her famous—that she was *paid* for—just because she was afraid of getting a C? They wouldn't understand at all. Some of them, like Bernice and Gloria, it occurred to her, might even think she had been fired from the paper.

I'll tell Miss Riker first, she thought. Then I'll just mention it to the girls.

The warmth in her teacher's eyes was her reward. "I'm so glad, Cathy! It really is the best thing. You know, I've been thinking. There's quite a bit of news that could be sent in from school. What is your editor's name?"

"Mr. Stark."

"Well, you're my good girl! Now you'll be my top student again!"

That helped. At recess she broke the news. Bernice and Gloria stared at her, completely unable to understand a girl who enjoyed such great importance and then just gave it up.

Bernice questioned her closely. "Did your mother and father make you give it up?"

"No."

"Did anybody?"

"No. I just decided."

"Why?"

"Because I don't have time to do my homework. And—other reasons."

They gazed at her, thinking her a curious creature indeed. But strangely Cathy sensed a kind of respect in their gaze. Dimly the realization came to her that by this very act she had once more set herself apart from the others. Without knowing that she did so, Cathy held her head higher.

Now she must break the news to Mr. Stark. Just a few weeks ago the editor would have been delighted to receive her resignation, she knew. Now she was not sure.

Mother, Grandma, Chris, and Jeff all came for her after school, and they drove into Springdale. It was Tuesday, and she had her copy—her final copy, rather slim this time—to deliver. When she went into the newspaper office Mr. Stark was sitting at his typewriter as usual.

But, what was most unusual, he greeted her by name. "Hello, Cathy."

It was warm in here. She pulled the scarf from her head and handed him the envelope. "I have to tell you something."

"Shoot."

"I have to stop working for you."

She waited for his reaction, but the editor merely leaned back in his chair and looked at her.

"Only I've got somebody else to do it, if you want her to, so I'm not letting you down."

"What brought this on?" the editor asked.

She told him as well as she could. "So, well, I just love being a reporter, but I hardly ever have time to play with my sister and brother and my friends. And I like to get good marks. I guess that's more important."

After a moment he nodded slowly. "You're right. Who've you got?"

"Mrs. Hughes. She's an author, so she knows how. Is that O.K.?"

"It's O.K." But his gaze still rested on her thoughtfully. "You know, Cathy," he said finally, "you're quite a society reporter."

He was making fun of her. She felt her

cheeks flush uncomfortably. Cathy said uncertainly, "Well, Mrs. Hughes will be very good, so. . . ."

"Nobody ever got so much news out of Middle Bridge before."

She stood speechless.

"I think you ought to know," the editor went on, "I've had quite a few new subscriptions from Middle Bridge since you've been on the job. I even got an ad."

Still Cathy stood there, unable to believe her ears.

"How would you like," Mr. Stark asked, "to send in news from your school?"

"From school?"

"Special programs, projects, class elections."

"I'd love to, only. . . ."

"You could do that in school hours. As a matter of fact, somebody suggested just this morning, and it seems like a good idea, that we appoint a junior correspondent in every school. Make it part of the regular schoolwork instead of writing—you know—essays and all that stuff. Good experience. How would you like that?"

"I'd love it!" Cathy gasped. "I've been just dying to write real news articles!"

"There's no money in it."

"I don't care!"

"O.K., you're a junior correspondent. We'll set it up after New Year's."

"Oh, Mr. Stark, thank you!" Cathy cried.

His eyes were actually twinkling. "You're welcome."

There seemed nothing more to add, so after a moment she moved toward the door. "Well, Merry Christmas," she said.

The next moment she couldn't help it. An overpowering impulse to do something to show him how thrilled and grateful she was rushed over Cathy. "Oh, Mr. Stark," she heard herself exclaim, "I want to give you a Christmas present! Wouldn't you like a darling little gray kitten named Independence?"

For a moment he stared at her blankly. And then the stern, disagreeable, unbending editor of the *Ferris County Crier* threw back his head and laughed. Cathy laughed, too, at herself, at him, at everything in the wonderful, joyous world.

"You needn't take her," she assured him

168

finally. "We want to get rid of her, so my sister can have a parakeet, but that *really* isn't the reason. I just wanted to give you. . . ."

"As a matter of fact," Mr. Stark said, "my wife has been craving a cat. Bring it in."

"I could hug you!" Cathy cried.

"Go along with you," he said. "Merry Christmas."

She left, walking on air. Oh, what a relief! For the first time she admitted the truth to herself. All those calls when she longed to be with Naomi or Chris or Jeff. And the hard, hard work of typing. No more. What a heavenly feeling. She could hardly believe she was free.

She thought suddenly, Miss Riker suggested that about junior correspondents. Now I can take all the time I need for homework, and I'll get a hundred in arithmetic every day! Yet the unbelievable had happened, and she was still a reporter, although a different kind.

She looked up as she felt the gossamer caress of a snowflake on her cheek. Above the Christmas lights strung across Main Street, unseen voices rang out: "God rest ye merry, gentlemen, let nothing you dismay."

There was nothing to dismay her now. Nothing.

Here was the car. They were all waiting expectantly for her, anxious to know how the editor had received her news. Cathy climbed into the car, conscious of a smile of perfect joy on her face, and settled back beside Grandma and Chris.

Only then did she say, "I'm a junior correspondent!"

And she threw her scarf over her happy face.